When Love Turns To Hate

By: Diamond Unique

Book Cover by Diamond Unique of BLK Sista Productions, LLC

1st edition 2025

ISBN: 979-8-218-60829-3

Trigger Warning

This book contains mature themes, including domestic violence and sexual assault. If you or someone you know has been affected by these issues, please seek help.
National Domestic Violence Hotline
1-800-799-7233
Please read with caution and take care of yourself.

Chapter 1

Tonight was the fucking night, Trap & Tease Friday was popping off, and the bass was booming through the speakers and I already knew tonight was about to get real. I was ready to get this money, and I knew the club was gonna be packed with all the right niggas and bitches looking to get lit.This shit was about to get wild, and I was ready to make my move, get paid, and leave with a fat stack of cash and a rich nigga on my arm.

That's when I met him. Marco. Fine as hell with chocolate skin, a gold chain glistening on his chest, and the walk like he owned the whole damn club. I was on stage at Club Moonlight Seductions, body moving to the beat like it was my last dance. The crowd was lit, throwing money like rent wasn't due next week. But I ain't even care about them. Not when I saw Marco sitting in VIP, sipping on some expensive-ass champagne, looking straight at me like I was dessert.

After my set, Passion came running up to me, all hyped. "Girl, dat dude in VIP wanna see you."

Normally I don't do that shit, but baby, I was curious. I strutted my thick ass over there, and Marco leaned back, licking his lips like I was a whole meal.

"Damn, you fine," he said, voice deep and smooth.

I smirked. "I know. What's your name, daddy?"

"Marco. And you?"

"Lyric." I responded.

He smiled. "Baby, you hit every note just right."

Chile, my knees got weak. We talked all night, his hand on my thigh, whispering in my ear like he already knew what was up. I ain't gonna lie-I was hooked from jump.

Fast forward six months, and I was Mrs. Marco Santana. Young, wild, and dumb in love. The sex was crazy, the money was flowing. Life was *perfect*. Or so I thought.

But that was just a dream, perfect turned toxic real quick. Marco started selling dope, and worse-*using it*. His kisses turned cold, and his hands...well, they weren't always soft anymore.

I love that man, but love ain't supposed to hurt like this. Or is it?

Let me tell you how it all started.

I'm Lyric. 22 years old, born and raised in the Eastside Projects. Grew up without a father, cause that man dipped before I could even say "daddy." My mama? She held it down. Worked herself to the max just to keep a roof over our heads and make sure I didn't want for nothing. I learned real quick that if you want something in this life, you don't wait for it to come to you-you go out and work for it. Ain't nobody handing you nothing, especially if you are a girl from the south, raised in the struggle.

Now? I'm at Club Moonlight Seductions, the hottest spot around the city. Strip club, yea. But it's more than that. This place? It's where I make money and where I call the shots. I walk that stage like a muthafuckin' boss, men throw cash, and I keep it moving. It ain't just a dance, it's about the power. I don't get touched unless I want to be. But last night? It was different. Last night changed everything.

I didn't think Marco was gonna come back. Thought he was just another guy, you know? Throw some cash, get a little show, and keep it moving. But no, he came back. Same VIP booth, eyes locked on me the second I hit the floor. I couldn't ignore it. Everytime I looked over, his stare was pulling me in like a damn magnet.

I wasn't about to play the "I don't care" game, though. I wasn't even trying to hide the fact that his energy was making my pulse race. I didn't expect it, but it was there. It was real.

So, let me spill the tea.

I finished my set, but instead of heading to back like usual, I slid straight to the bar, grabbed a drink, and kept my eyes on him. Didn't matter who else was looking. I was focused. He was looking at me like he wanted more than just a show.

And I wasn't about to leave it there. I grabbed my courage, walked right to that VIP section, and I sat down right next to him. No hesitation. I wasn't the type to play games or pretend I wasn't feeling the same heat he was throwing my way.

"You back again?" I asked, raising an eyebrow. I didn't need to say much. He was already hooked.

He didn't smile at first, but there was something in the way his eyes softened. "Yeah. I came back for you," he said, and his voice? Damn. It hit different. "Last night, dat dance…it wasn't like anything I've ever seen."

I leaned back in the seat, trying to hide the way the words sent a little spark through me. "Is that right?" I said, giving him a slow smile, not letting him see how much I was into this whole thing.

"Hell yeah. You move different. Like you know exactly what I need before I do." His eyes never left mine, that look steady and intense. "I need to see if this is real."

The challenge was there. The pull between us? Real. I wasn't stupid. I could feel it too. But I wasn't here to give him everything just because he showed up again. I wasn't that easy. So, I stood up, did a slow turn, and started heading toward the stage.

He followed me with his eyes, and I didn't need to look back to know it. The energy between us was undeniable. When I hit that pole, I didn't just dance for the crowd. I dance for him. Every move I made was for him to see.

I didn't treat him like others. This wasn't about the money, the tips, the regular show...Nah. This was about showing him a side of me that nobody else got to see. I wasn't just a body on stage. I was everything.

When I finished, I walked right back to him, not breaking eye contact. He was already standing there waiting, that smirk on his face telling me he was feeling it, too. I didn't waste time tonight. I slid right into his lap, slow and easy, like it was the most natural thing to do in the world.

His hands rested on my waist, but he didn't pull me closer. He let me do it. Let me lead. And for once, I didn't mind. His eyes were on me, focused, as if he wanted to see what I would do next.

When the song ended, I slid off him like nothing happened, but damn, I felt the tension thick between us. He didn't say anything at first, just watched me. And I knew he was trying to figure out what the hell just happened.

"Yo' you something else, Lyric," he finally said, his voice rougher than it was before. "I can't keep my eyes off you."

I smirked, wiping my forehead, acting cool like I wasn't just hooked as he was. "Told you, baby. I ain't like the rest."

That was it. Just like that, the game had changed. He was part of something else now. Marco wasn't just another man in the club. He was something special, but I didn't know I was gonna fall for him that fast, but I sure as hell wasn't turning away. And the way he looked at me? He knew it too.

Tonight? Yeah, tonight was just the beginning.

The air between us was heavy now, thick with something deeper. I could feel it in my veins, the tension sparking between us like it was about to explode. Marco was sitting there, staring at me like I was the only thing in the room, and that's when I knew I had him.

I stood up slowly, giving him just enough time to catch the curves of my hips, to see the way I moved like I owned the whole damn room. My body was my weapon, and tonight? I was aiming it right at him.

I didn't look back when I headed to the bar, but I knew Marco's eyes were glued to me, following my every step. And when I grabbed that drink, I could feel the heat of his stare still burning through me.

I turned around, locking eyes with him, and the smile I gave him wasn't innocent. I wasn't acting shy, I wasn't trying to hold back. I was letting him see all of me...the real me. I didn't care who knew I wanted him , long as he wanted me too.

"So, what you got planned tonight?" I said, being flirty.

Marco leaned forward, his eyes still on me, like he was trying to read me. "I was hoping you'd tell me," he said, his voice low, like he wasn't just asking about tonight...he was asking everything.

I grinned, walking back over to him slow, every step calculated, my hips swaying just enough to keep him interested. I slid into the seat next to him, close enough to feel his heat, but still giving him that space to wonder just how far I was willing to go.

"Well," I said, letting the words roll off my tongue, "Hopefully, you're going home with me tonight."

I put my hand behind his head, my eyes never leaving he's, making sure he knew I wasn't saying it just to tease. I was saying it because it was real. Because I wasn't about to waste time pretending I wasn't feeling the same pull he was.

He looked at me for a second, like he was trying to hold it together, but I could see it. That shift in his gaze. The little fire burning behind his eyes.

"You think you can just walk in here and tell me dat?" he asked, his lips curling into a slight smirk while he licked his lips.

I leaned in closer, close enough for him to feel my breath against his skin, but still keeping it cool. "I don't think. I know."

The tension in his body told me everything I needed to know. He wasn't backing down. And neither was I.

Marco reached up, brushing his hand along the side of my arm, a move so casual but so damn charged it sent a shiver through me.

"I guess we'll see what happens then," he said, barely above a whisper.

I smiled, the kind of smile that said I was ready to take control. "You damn right we will," I responded.

I wasn't about to play the waiting game anymore. The night was still young, but I could already tell this was about to go somewhere neither of us expected. I was ready for whatever the night was about to throw at me, Maybe I was going to be throwing it at him.

Chapter 2

The club was winding down, the lights were flickering like they were catching the same vibe. I was tired but restless, ready for something more. My shift was almost over, but there was this buzz, like the whole night had been leading to this one moment.

Marco.

I glanced over at the bar. He was still there, watching me like he was waiting for something. Or maybe *someone*. And I knew damn well who that was.

I grabbed my jacket from the back, flicking my hair out one time in the mirror. This wasn't gonna be no regular night. I could feel my body feening for him, and the chemistry was thick as hell. It was more than just the heat from the club; this man had my pussy throbbing so bad I felt like I was gonna cum at any moment. And I wasn't even going to cap, I wanted him so bad, so I already knew it was going down.

I walked toward him, heels clicking, ass bouncing, just enough for him to notice. When I saw his eyes following me, I couldn't help but to smile. He didn't know whether to pull me in or let me come to him, but either way, he was about to get me.

When I stood right in front of him, I leaned in close, not saying a word at first. Just letting the silence settle in, the air thick with what was about to happen. Then, I broke it. "Come on, daddy," I whispered, voice sexy, smooth and teasing. "You ready to see how this night really ends?"

I watched as his gaze darkened, a shift in him like he couldn't hold back no more. His hands reached out, slow but sure, like he knew exactly what he wanted. "I'm waiting on you ma," he muttered, his voice so deep, like he was trying to make love to me right here.

That was all I needed to hear. No more words. I grabbed his hand and pulled him up, guiding him out the booth and through the back door, leaving the noise of the club behind. Just me and him now, the rest of the world outside. We walked down the alley, it was like we were the only two people left on Earth. We hopped in his car and he drove me to my place. Slow R&b music playing on the radio and city lights just make it more romantic.

When we finally made it to my place, my luxury one-bedroom apartment that I worked damn hard for. I could see the surprise in his eyes. Not that I needed to say anything. My place spoke for itself-clean, modern, with views of the city lights flickering in the distance. It wasn't flashy, but it was mine.

I kicked off my heels and walked straight to the kitchen, grabbing a bottle of champagne, uncorking it with a flick of the wrist. I poured us both a drink, sliding it over to him, and when his fingers brushed mine, the spark was undeniable. His touch sent a jolt straight to my chest.

He didn't speak right away, just looked at me, like he was trying to figure me out, but I wasn't giving him that easy streak...not tonight.

I stepped closer, close enough for him to feel the heat coming off me. I wasn't trying to hide the energy between us anymore.

"You want me, don't you?" I asked, voice low, almost a whisper.

He stepped to me, closing the distance until his lips were close to my ear. "You already know how I'm feeling," he said, his breath warm, sending chills down my spine.

And that was it. Everything shifted in that moment.

I stood up, walking toward the kitchen and that's when Marco grabbed me by my hips and started kissing me. As Marco's lips glazed my neck, I felt shivers run down my spine. It was like my body was already attached to him.

Ahh, damn, Marco bent me the fuck over, stroking me slowly and making my pussy curve to his dick. He started stroking me harder and his dick was slamming into my pussy. It felt like he was trying to break something. I'm talking about deep strokes. He got me hollering & screaming and shit.

He's grabbing my waist, pulling me back onto his dick like he owns me or something. And I'm loving every minute of it, ain't no denying that. My pussy getting wetter by the second, juices dripping down my thighs like a faucet that won't turn off.

Marco's breath on my neck, his lips on my skin, making me shiver like a bitch. He's eating my pussy out like it's his favorite meal on the menu, tongue dancing across my clit like he's trying to make me squirt all on him. "I'm cumming, I cumming!" I said, and he just kept on going, ain't no stopping.

Now he flips me over , face down ass up, and Marco's fucking me from behind like an animal. His hands on my hips, pulling me back onto his dick with each stroke. My titties are bouncing, and my ass is shaking, and Marco just keeps pounding.

He slapped my ass so hard, it stung for a minute but then the pain turned into pleasure and now I want more of that shit. So I started talking dirty to him "slap it again daddy", then Marco started going crazy slapping both cheeks talking about "You like dat?", all I could scream was "Yesss Daddy".

Marco starts to slow down a lil bit then speeds back up again. I can tell he was about to cum by the way he moaning and grunting and breathing heavy. He grips my hips tighter than before and then I felt him swell up inside me, then he let out one last thrust, "Baby I'm bout to bust," he yelled. He bust, I came at the same damn time, the feeling had my damn toes curled up, then we both just collapse onto the bed exhausted but satisfied, and I loved every damn moment of it.

I looked at Marco with a curious expression, "Where do we go from this point?" I asked, my voice barely above a whisper. Marco smiled, his eyes locked on mine, and said, "I guess this makes you my lady now."

I raised my eyebrow, a shy grin spreading across my face, "Is that so?" I replied, my tone playful. Marco nodded, his smile growing wider. "Yeah, that's so," he said, his voice low and husky.

Just then, Marco's phone rang, he glanced at the screen and his expression turned serious. "I got to go handle some business," he said, already getting out of bed. I nodded, watching as he quickly got dressed.

I stayed in bed, just wrapped up in a sheet, feeling the warmth of our encounter still radiating from my skin. Marco came over and gave me a quick kiss on the forehead before heading to the door.

I got up, with the sheet still around me and walked him to the door. "Be careful out there," I said. Marco nodded and gave me another kiss before stepping out into the night.

As soon as the door closed behind him, I let out a sigh and headed to the shower. The warm water cascaded down my skin as I started to reminisce about our love making. I thought about the way Marco had touched me, the way he had made me feel like I was the only woman in the world for him.

I closed my eyes, letting the water wash away all my worries and doubts. For a moment, I just let myself feel like letting go of all of my fears. As I stood there, lost in thought, I couldn't help but wonder what would happen next between us.

The sound of the water was soothing, but my mind was racing with thoughts of

Marco and what our future might hold. I thought about all the things we had talked about earlier that night…where we were going from here, would we be together or keep it casual?

As I rinsed off and stepped out of the shower, I felt refreshed but also uncertain about what tomorrow would bring for us.

But little did I know, this man would soon trap me in a world of abuse and fear with no escaping from his control.

I woke up the next morning, feeling like a queen, and headed to the kitchen to whip up some breakfast. As I was scrambling some eggs and toasting some bread, my phone rang. It was my ride or die, Karmen.

"Girl Wassup," I said when I answered the phone.

"Yaaas bitch, what's good?" Karmen asked in her voice all extra and loud.

"Ain't nothin much, I'm just making me some breakfast," I replied, trying to sound all casual and whatnot.

"So, spill the tea," Karmen said, her tone turnt up a notch. "What happened at the club last night?"

I hesitated for a hot second before responding, "I met this dude Marco, "I said, trying to gauge Karmen's reaction.

Karmen sucked her teeth on the other end of the line. "Uh-uh, Lyric, I don't know about dat, Lyric, I don't know about this one," she said, her voice all skeptical and whatnot. "You know I don't like nobody trying to hurt you, you're my sis, and I got your back."

I knew Karmen was coming from a real place. She had been with me through thick and thin, and she had seen me get played by other dudes in the past. But I tried to explain myself to Karmen.

"Karmen, listen...Marco is really different, he is a real gentleman, and he swag is on point." I said.

But Karmen wasn't having it. She let out a laugh on the other end of the line. "Girl bye! You like him cause he got swag and he can sweet talk you with his lies? Nah! He earned you! He got you right where he wants you!"

Karmen's words cut deep. I knew she was looking out for me but sometimes she could be too extra.

"Karmen chill out!" I snapped back at her. "You don't even know him!"

But Karmen kept going, not holding back nothing. "Earned you!" she repeated again for emphasis. "Girl that man got his hooks in you already! Mark my words...he's gone mess with your head until it spins around like crazy!"

I sighed heavily into the phone...knowing that sometimes my best friend could be right...but also way too dramatic at times.

"Karmen, I got to go," I said, trying to wrap up the conversation. "I'll talk to you later, okay?" Karmen agreed, but not before throwing in one last warning:

"Just be careful, lyric. Don't say I didn't warn you."

I hung up the phone and stood there for a moment. Is she right or is she just jealous of me? I couldn't shake that shit off, but in due time I would find out the truth.

Chapter 3

As I sat in my apartment, sipping on a cup of coffee and enjoying the quiet morning, my mind began to wander to Marco. We had just started dating, and I was really feeling him, but I hadn't heard from him all morning. I decided to send him a text, just to see what was going on. "Hey baby, wyd? I'm bored chilling at my place."

He responded quickly, "Hey baby, I'm at work right now, but I'll call you later." Okay sounds good, I thought. But now that I had nothing to do, I was getting a little bored. So, I decided to get dressed and head out to the mall. I put on my new red Nike dress and slipped on my red bottoms - it was time to treat myself. I got my keys and got in my car and drove to the mall.

As I approached the mall, I saw a sign that there is a new clothing store that just opened. I got out of my car and walked into the mall. As I walked into the mall, I glanced over to my right and saw the new store Fly Girl Boutique.

I walked into the store and all the new fashion designer clothes were in there. I decided to just browse a little bit and check out the prices. As I looked around, I couldn't help but notice a girl staring at me from across the room. Her name tag said Keke, and she looked like she had something on her mind.

"Can I help you find something?" Keke asked, walking over to me with a curious expression.

"Nah, I'm good, just browsing," I replied, trying to brush her off.

But Keke wasn't having it. "So, what brings you in here today?" she asked, leaning against the rack next to me.

I shrugged my shoulders, "Just looking for something new, I guess. You know how it is."

Keke nodded. "Yeah, I do. So do you come to the mall often?"

I laughed. "Yeah, but it's been a while. But I've heard great things about this store before y'all open."

Keke smiled. "Well, we try our best to keep our customers happy. So, what do you think of our selection so far?"

I scanned the room quickly before responding. "It's nice. You guys have some really cute stuff."

Just as I was about to ask Keke a question about one of the dresses on the rack, she dropped a bombshell on me.

"Hey, can I ask you something?" Keke said with a serious expression.

"Sure," I replied cautiously.

"Do you know a guy name Marco?" she asked point-blank.

My heart skipped a beat as soon as she mentioned his name…why is this girl asking about Marco?

"Yeah…why are you asking me about him?"

"Oh girl…where do I even begin? Did he tell you he got a baby on the way?!?!"

My eyes widened in shock and anger started rising up inside of me…What the hell?!

"No! He didn't tell me that! Who are you? How do you even know him?! And more importantly, who's having his damn baby?!"

I stood there, my eyes fixed on Keke, waiting for her to explain what was going on.

"Okay, so… Marco and I, we've been talking for almost 6 months now," Keke said, her voice shaking slightly. "We met through mutual friends and hit it off right away. We've been seeing each other ever since, and I saw your photo on his phone the other night."

I felt a knot in my stomach as I listened to Keke's words. This couldn't be happening.

"So, you're saying that you are pregnant by Marco?" I asked, trying to keep my cool.

Keke nodded, tears welling up in her eyes. "Yes, that's right. We've been together for a while now and... well you know how things get."

I took a deep breath, trying to process everything that was happening. This was too much to handle.

"How could he not tell me about you?" I demanded, my voice rising. "How could he not tell me that he had a baby on the way?"

Keke shrugged. "I don't know, Girl. Maybe he was just trying to keep it from you. Maybe he didn't want you to know about me."

That's when I lost it.

"Are you fucking kidding me?!" I exclaimed, my voice echoing through the store. "He's been playing me this whole muthafuckin' time? He's been lying to me and cheating on me with you?"

Keke looked scared by my outburst. "Girl, calm down..."

But I wasn't having it.

"No, fuck that! You're telling me that the man I've been dating is having a baby with you? That's some messed up shit! He's a damn liar and a cheat!"

The store fell silent as everyone turned to stare at us.

"So let me ask you this," I asked. "Are you and him still dating?"

Keke paused with fear in her eyes. "Yes," she answered. "'I'm sorry," Keke said, looking like she was about to cry.

But I wasn't interested in her apologies.

"Sorry? Sorry isn't enough! You need to stay the fuck away away from him. I don't believe shit you say!," I yelled.

With that, I turned around and stormed out of the store."This is some bullshit!" I muttered under my breath as I walked away from the boutique. As soon as I got outside, I pulled out my phone and dialed Marco's number. His phone rang.

"Yo, whats up baby," he answered.

"Don't baby me," I yelled. Why you ain't tell me you had another girl?"

"What!," he said. "Okay lyric, what are you talking about baby?"

"Don't play dumb with me, Marco!" I screamed, my anger boiling over. "I just got done talking to Keke, and she told me everything. You're having a baby with her and everything." So tell me, is it true?"

Marco blew on the other end of the line. "Lyric, calm down and let me explain..."

But I wasn't having it.

"Explain? Explain what? How you've been lying to me this whole time? How you already got a girl named Keke?"

"Lyric, it's not like that," Marco said, his voice rising. "Keke and I, we have a history together. We were together before I met you, and...well, things happened.

"A history together?" I repeated, my voice incredulous. "You mean like a romantic story? Because that's sure what it sounds like."

Marco hesitated before responding. "Yes, Lyric. Keke and I were in a relationship before I met you. But it was over between us months ago."

"Bullshit!" I exclaimed. "If it was over between you two, then why is she saying she pregnant with your child and don't look like she is nothing but a few weeks.

There was a pause on the other end of the line before Marco responded.

"Look, Lyric. I know this is a lot to take in. but please just listen to me and try to understand..."

But I wasn't interested in understanding.

"No, Marco! You need to listen to me! You're a lying ass nigga. You've been playing me this whole time, using me for your own entertainment while you're still involved with Keke!"

"That's bullshit!" Marco shouted back at me. "You're being dramatic and unreasonable! You don't even know the whole story!"

"I don't need to know the whole story!" I yelled back at him. "What I do know is that you're a dishonest piece of shit who couldn't even tell the truth! And as for being dramatic and unreasonable…fuck you! You have no right to talk about how I'm behaving when you're the one who's been lying.

The conversation had devolved into a full-blown screaming match by now.

"Just leave me alone Marco!" I shouted finally. You don't have to worry about me anymore, focus on your woman and your child you created," and I hung up the phone.

Walking out of the mall, tears streaming down my face, I was hurt. I couldn't believe that motherfucka had been playing me like that. I got to my car and just started banging on the steering wheel, trying to get all my emotions out.

As I was driving back home, Marco's name kept popping up on my phone. He was blowing me up, trying to get me to answer. But I was done with his ass. I ain't got time for no lying nigga.

I pulled up to my apartment and just went straight to my room. I laid across the bed, feeling like shit. Why did this happen to me? Why did he have to play me like that?

I picked up my phone and called my mom, crying like a baby.

"Momma it's over," I sobbed into the phone. "He was cheating on me with some other bitch and she's pregnant!"

My mom listened patiently as I told her everything that happened.

"That man ain't worth your tears, baby," she said. "You deserve so much better than someone who's gonna play you like that."

I nodded in agreement, even though she couldn't see me.

Just then, Marco's name popped up on my phone again. "Lord, why do he keep on calling me?" I asked my mom.

"Don't answer it, baby," she said firmly. "You don't need him right now."

"I'm just going to lay down a little bit mom, my head is hurting, I will call you back a little later, I love you," I said.

"I love you baby," mom said before she hung up the phone.

After hanging up with my mom, Marco kept calling, I decided to answer it just to give him a piece of my mind.

"What the fuck do you want, Marco?" I spat into the phone as soon as he answered.

"Chill with how you talking to me," Marco said calmly. "I know you're upset..."

"Upset?" I cut him off. "You think? You played me like a fool and now you're tryna act all innocent?"

Marco sighed on the other end of the line.

"Lyric, Listen to me...can I please just come talk to you face to face?"

"No!" I shouted into the phone. "We ain't got talk about shit. You made your bed now lie in it with your baby mama!"

Marco tried to respond but I cut him off again.

"I'm done with your ass! Tonight when I get ready for work at the club imma make sure I look so good that every nigga there gone take care of me...Not you tho!"

With that said, I hung up on his ass for good.

I picked up my phone and dialed Passion's number to inform her about tonight.

"Hey girl, wassup?" Passion answered on the first ring.

"Not much, just getting ready for tonight," I replied, trying to sound casual despite the emotional rollercoaster I'd been on earlier.

"Okay, cool. So, what's the plan for tonight?" Passion asked.

"I want to do the pole show tonight," I said firmly. "And I want to make sure it's something real sexy. I got a new lingerie set that's gonna kill it."

Passion squealed on the other end of the line. "Yaaas, girl! That sounds amazing! What song do you want to dance to?"

I was thinking of the Beyonce song "Dance for You," I replied. "Something that'll get the crowd going and make me feel like a queen."

Passion agreed and we started discussing the details of the show. But then she asked, "Girl, what's wrong? You sound a little off."

I sighed, not wanting to get into it over the phone. "I'll explain everything when I get to the club, okay? Just make sure everything is good for tonight."

Passion was quiet for a moment before responding. "Aight, girl, everything's gon be ok, don't worry, I'll have you looking and feeling like a million bucks."

I smiled slightly, feeling grateful for my friend's support. "Thanks, Passion. I owe you one."

We chatted for a few more minutes before hanging up. As soon as we did, Marco's name popped up on screen again. But I ignored it and focused on getting ready for tonight's show instead.

It was time to put Marco behind me and focus on myself for a change. As I looked in the mirror while singing along with the radio. It's on tonight, I'm really going to smile because I deserve to be happy.

Little do y'all know this night is going to be one of the worst nights of my life. Just know that everything that glitters ain't gold.

Chapter 4

I walked into the strip club, the music and lights immediately hyping me up. It was going to be a big night, and I could feel the energy in the air like a live wire. I made my way to the back, where I quickly changed into my sexy lingerie. The outfit was everything I had hoped for - it hugged my curves in all the right places and made me feel like a million bucks, honey.

As I finished getting ready, Passion came over to give me a pep talk. "Girl, you got this! You look sexy as fuck tonight, boo. You're gonna kill it out there tonight! Show'em what you workin with!"

I smiled, feeling a surge of confidence. "I know I am," I replied, taking a shot of liquor to calm my nerves. The burn of the liquor went down smooth, and I felt my fears melt away.

The DJ's voice boomed through the speakers, announcing my stage name: "Coming to stage right now, If ya'll like to make it rain, get them dollars ready for Storm!"

I took a deep breath, walked onto the stage and grabbed my pole and started climbing the pole and twirling with my legs in the air like I owned the place. The crowd erupted into cheers as I began to dance, my body moving in perfect sync with the music. My hips swirled, my ass shook, and my tits bounced to the beat. Dollar bills were flying everywhere.

As I glanced out in the audience, my eyes scanned the crowd until they landed on one person-Marco. He wa sitting in the front row, looking mad as fuck. But I didn't give a damn about him or his drama tonight. Tonight was about me, and me alone.

I focused on my dance, pouring all my energy into it. The crowd went wild as I spun and twirled around the pole, shaking my ass and showing off my skills. My lingerie sparkled under the lights, and my hair flew around me like a halo.

As I danced, I could feel Marco's eyes on me, but I refused to let him get under my skin. Instead, I used his presence as fuel for my performance. I danced harder and sexier than ever before, determined to show him what he was missing.

The crowd loved every minute of it, clapping and screaming and chanting "Storm! Strom!" as they threw money onto the stage. Dollars rained down around me like confetti.

When it was all over and I walked off the stage, Passion ran up behind me, giving me hugs and slapping my ass, telling me how proud she was that I got my own shit together tonight despite Marco showing up.

"Yaaas girl you killed that shit!" Passion screamed while hugging me from behind.

"I told you I would," I replied while laughing.

As me and Passion started walking away, Marco approached me, his eyes glassy and unfocused. He was swaying slightly, and his speech was slurred.

"Wha's good, Lyric?" he asked, his voice dripping with a condescending tone. "You think you're all high and mighty just 'cause you're up on that stage, don't you?"

I raised an eyebrow, focused on his rudeness. "What's wrong with you, Marco?" I asked, my tone firm. "You seem like you're on something."

Marco laughed, a cold, mirthless sound. "I'm just fine, baby," he said, his words dripping with sarcasm. "I'm just trying to have a conversation with you."

But it was clear that he was not fine. He was stumbling over his words, and his eyes kept darting back and forth like he was searching for something.

"Look, Marco," I said firmly. "I don't know what's going on with you right now, but I don't have time for this shit. You need to get your shit together before you try to talk to me."

Marco sneered at me, his face twisted in a snarl. "You think you're too good for me?" he said. "You think you're the queen just 'cause you're shaking your ass on stage?"

I felt a surge of anger at his words, but I kept my cool. "I'm not too good for anyone," I said calmly. "But I am too good for someone who is clearly addicted to drugs and got a baby on the way."

Marco's face turned red with rage, and he took a step closer to me. But before he could say anything else, passion stepped in and grabbed my arm.

"Girl, do you need me to throw this fuck nigga out the club?" she yelled in anger.

"Nahh, I'm good girl," I said with a smirk, "This nigga clearly on something and I don't let this kind of drama get to me."

"Ok," Passion said, and we turned to walk away from Marco once again.

Marco's face realized he wasn't getting anywhere with me. He yelled and said "Lyric hold on real quick," with a slur. I turned around and looked at him but before he could get his words out, his phone started ringing. I shock my head.

"Nahh, you might wanna handle your fucking business first," I suggested.

Marco tried to brush it off. "This is work," he said. "I'll be back."

But I wasn't focused on him.

"Yeah, you said that shit last time," I reminded him. "And now you've got a baby on the way? Miss me with that bullshit."

I turned to walk but not before delivering one final blow.

"I got bands to run up," I said over my shoulder. "Marco you not worth my time no more, Fuck out my face. "You're nothing but a cheating ass nigga and I don't need your sorry ass in my life."

Marco stormed out the club, looking all mad and shit, but I ain't never been one to sweat no nigga. I walked up to the bar, ordered myself a shot, and was just relaxing myself.

Then, out of nowhere, this fine dude walks up to me. He was looking good as fuck, with them piercing brown eyes and them juicy lips. He had on a fitted white shirt and some dark blue jeans, and he looked like he just stepped out of a magazine or something.

"Yo, what's good?" he asked me, with a smile that could light up a room.

"I'm good," I replied, smiling back at him.

"My name Sincere," he said, "But everybody calls me Sin."

"I'm Lyric," I said back, shaking his hand, "but everyone here calls me Storm."

Sin looked at me with them cat colored eyes that seemed to see right through me. "Can I buy you a drink?" he asked.

I nodded my head, and he ordered us both a drink. We sat there for a minute, sipping on our drinks and vibing, before he spoke up again.

"I wasn't all in your business," he said, "But I seen you talking to that other nigga earlier. And let me tell you something, Lyric...I would never do you like that."

I raised my eyebrow while I looked at him. "All ya'll niggas say the same shit," I said skeptically.

But Sin just smiled at me with them grillz in his mouth. "Ma," he said softly...all dudes ain't the same".

And Lord have mercy...I blushed like crazy...

"How about we get more personal then?" He suggested.

"How personal?" I responded.

"Private dance," He said.

"It's 200." I stated.

He nodded and just smiled at me, "Ok bet," and I was ok with that. I grabbed his hand and I led the way and said, "Let me take you to paradise baby."

I took Sincere back to the private room and gave him the best lap dance of his life. The men couldn't touch us, but I let him feel on me and his hands were just what I needed. I felt things getting a little too heated, so I stopped it.

"I'm just getting out of something," I told him, trying to explain. "I don't want to put myself back in something like that."

Sincere nodded understandingly. "Just take my number," he said. "If you need anything, I'm a call away."

I smiled as he looked at me and gave me the money. We left the VIP room and he grabbed my hand.

"I'm serious," he said, looking at me with piercing greenish eyes. "If you need anything, don't be afraid. Just because one nigga fucked up doesn't mean all of us are like that."

I was blushing and feeling all kinds of things, but little did I know, Marco was back and he saw us together. He came up to me and grabbed my arm, his face twisted with anger.

"Lyric, what the fuck is this?" he demanded. "What you doing with this bitch ass nigga?"

Sincere stepped forward, his eyes flashing with anger, "Nigga, first of all don't be grabbing on her like that," as he stared him dead in his face. "You on the wrong side of town," Sincere said calmly.

I was confused and asking what was going on? But Marco just kept talking.

"This nigga and his crew trying to take my turf," he said.

"Turf?" I repeated, laughing in disgust. "Marco, you a drug dealer! You can't even take care of yourself!"

The situation escalated quickly and before I knew it, everything went left. Marco and Sincere started throwing punches, the bouncer came over and grabbed me out of the way just in time as they crashed into a table.

As they kept on fighting, the bouncers finally managed to separate them by putting both of them in a chicken wing hold from behind.

As they were being dragged outside by security, Marco's eye's looked onto mine, his face twisted with rage.

"Lyric this ain't over wit!," He yelled.

I was so shaken up by that bullshit, I ran to the back of the club, trying to process everything that had just happened. Passion ran to the back after me, so concerned about me.

"Girl, are you ok?" She asked, checking on me.

I just burst into tears, unable to hold it in anymore. "Do someone got a curse on me or something?" I cried, feeling like my life was spiraling out of control.

Passion looked at me like she was about to cry too. "Bitch, I don't know," she said. "But what's going on with you and Marco? Why the hell did he come up here anyway?"

I shook my head, feeling frustrated and overwhelmed. "I don't know," I said. "I'm just done with tonight. I'm going home."

Passion nodded in understanding. "Okay, girl. But you can't just leave like that. That crazy muthafucka might be outside waiting for you."

I didn't care at this point. I just wanted to go home and forget about everything that had happened tonight.

"I'll be back tomorrow night," I said, grabbing my things.

Passion looked at me with a concern in her eyes. "Well let me get one of the bouncers to walk you to your car," she said. "I don't want you going out there alone with Marco possibly waiting for you."

I nodded, feeling a sense of relief wash over me. Maybe having a bouncer walk me to my car would make me feel safer.

As we walked out of the club, Passion by my side and a bouncer leading the way. I couldn't help but feel like my life was about to get more complicated.

"Girl, you need to be careful," Passion said as we reached my car. "Marco ain't no joke."

I nodded in agreement as the bouncer opened my car door for me.

"I'll be fine," I said, trying to sound confident.

But deep down, I knew that nothing was fine right now.
And then Passion whispered, "Bitch, Marco got connections."

I got in my car and drove home, feeling like I was about to break down. Tonight had been a whole mess, and I just wanted to take a hot shower, lay down, and watch some tv ro calm my damn nerves. As I walked into my apartment, I felt a sense of relief was over me. I was finally alone and could relax.

I went into my room to get some clothes out for my shower and was about to head to the bathroom when I heard a knock at the door. I sighed, wondering who the fuck it could be. I walked over to the door and said, "Who is it?"

"It's Marco," he replied.

I hesitated for a moment, wondering what the hell he wanted. "What do you want?" I asked him.

"I just wanna talk," he said. "I wanna apologize and explain myself."

I felt like he had calmed down, so I opened the door and let him in. We walked into the living room and sat down. But Marco wasn't there for what he said he was there for.

As soon as we sat down, his face expression changed. He looked all angry and shit again.

"Lyric, what the fuck were you doing with Sin tonight?" he asked, his voice all aggressive.

"That's none of your fucking business," I responded back. "What do you want? You got another girl and a baby on the way, so why are you even here?"

He responded with some more bullshit.

"Did you fuck him back there?"

Chapter 5

Marco was not making the night any better, I got all defensive and told him, "I don't owe you no explanation for shit! You ain't my damn daddy! I don't have to tell you nothing!"

I already knew this conversation was going left, so I stood up and told Marco to get the fuck outta my apartment.

He said, "I ain't going nowhere until you tell me what yall did!"

And then he started getting angry again.

"You mad 'cause Sin was getting attention from me?" I responded.

Marco got even angrier after that.

"This shit ain't me!" Get the fuck outta my house Marco!" I yelled.

Marco then grabbed my arm again. "Get the fuck off of me nigga!" I said.

Then Marco looked at me and said, "That nigga ain't yo man, and If I can't have you nobody can." I looked Marco dead and his face and said, "Fuck you Marco!" and I meant that shit.Then before I knew it Marco had slapped me across the fucking floor.

I was laid out on the floor, my mind messed up, trying to process the fact that this nigga Marco had just put his hands on me. My lip was throbbing, bleeding, and I could feel the pain radiating through my face.

Marco came over to me, looking all sorry and shit, but I ain't wanna hear it "Baby, I'm sorry," he said, his voice all shaky and weak.

But I was too busy crying, too busy trying to figure out why this man would do some shit like this. "Why you hit me, Marco?" I asked him, my voice all cracked and emotional. "What's wrong with you?"

Marco just kept saying the same ol' thing over and over again. "Bae, I fucked up. I'm sorry."

But that ain't enough for me. I need more than just some empty apologies.

Just then, Karmen burst through the door, her eyes wide with anger and concern. "Lyric, you okay girl?" she asked me. Not even knowing that Karmen had been texting me letting me know she was coming over so that we could talk.

Then she saw Marco standing there, looking all guilty and shit.

"Muthafucka, I know you ain't put your hands on her," she said to him.

Karmen pulled out a gun from her purse and pointed it straight at Marco. "Get the fuck outta here," she growled.

Marco Still trying to apologize and shit as he backed away from me. "Lyric baby I'm sorry," he muttered. But all I could do is stare at him, frozen in shock as he leaves.

I couldn't do nothing but cry, holding my face in my hands. I was shocked, in disbelief that Marco, the man I trusted , had turned around and hurt me. I thought he was coming over to talk, to apologize and make things right, but instead he put his hands on me.

Karmen came over to me, her voice soft and gentle. "I'm sorry, Lyric," she said. "Glad something told me to come over tonight. Girl I was about to put 12 rounds in his ass if he didn't leave."

I just shook my head, tears streaming down my face. I couldn't believe what had just happened. Karmen sat down next to me and put her arm around me. "Girl I can't stand to see you like this," she said.

I just shooked my head, still trying to process all this shit. But all I could do was cry from being hurt. I mean that night we made love, this man had me feeling like he was going to change my life and sweep me off my feet. I guess I was wrong.

After a few minutes of sitting there in silence, I finally spoke up. "Karmen...can I stay at your place tonight?" I asked, my voice barely above a whisper.

Karmen nodded immediately. "Of course, girl," she said. "You can stay with me as long as you need."I nodded again, feeling a little better knowing that I had somewhere safe to go. As we sat there for a few more minutes, karmen's phone started ringing. She got up to answer it and walked into the other room.

I got up off the floor, and was trying to figure out why Karmen go into the room and closed the door. She has never been a secretive person around me, I was like "What the fuck is this bitch doing? Why she going in the room to talk on the phone?" Something just ain't seem right, so I stood by the door to listen. And what I heard made my blood boil.

"Marco, what the fuck was I suppose to do? It was on yo ass to tell her," Karmen said.

I was like, "What the fuck is going on here? Why is this bitch talking to Marco?"

Then I heard her say, "Well, that's my best friend and I didn't expect this to happen."

And Marco was still talkin' on the other end, telling her something. And then she said,

"I love you too." That's when I busted into the room.

"Bitch, you ain't shit!" I said. "You been seeing Marco this whole time and we suppose to be best friends?"

Karmen looked at me like a deer with headlights on. "Lyric, I'm so sorry," she said. "It wasn't even nothing like that. He came to me and asked me how to win you back."

I wasn't even feeling that shit. "He came to you and asked you how to win me back and then what?" I asked.

"We were both drinking and one thing led to another," Karmen stated.

I was angry and hurt right now. Why would my best friend do this to me?

"Bitch, get out!" I said finally.

Karmen looked at me all sad and shit. "Lyric please," she said. But I was done listening to anything she had to say.

"You ain't got nothing else to say to me! I yelled. You can leave my house now."

She just put her head down and picked up her keys off the floor. She walked straight to the door after lookin' back at me slowly. And then she closed the door behind her.

I just stood there for a minute, feeling like my world had been turned upside down. First Macro put his hands on me and now my best friend had been secretly seeing him behind my back.

"What's wrong with these muthafuckas?" I asked myself out loud.

I walked to my room and decided to finish my night off with relaxation. I grabbed my sexy pajamas, ran some warm water & added some bubble bath, poured myself a glass of champagne & put some smooth jazz music on. As I soaked in the tub, I couldn't help but to think about Marco. Why did he hit me? All them memories came flashing back. Him cheating on me, lying to me and not one time did we make up.

I thought we were good, but obviously not. After being in the tub for a while, I grabbed my towel and dried off and put my pajamas on. I glanced at my phone on the bed and saw that Marco had called me 22 times.

"This muthafucka must think I'm crazy" I thought to myself. But I was still in love with him, why? I don't know. It was something about the way he made me feel. I just couldn't put my hands on it.

I sat there on my bed, staring at my phone, thinking about the times Marco had called me. I thought to myself, "Next time he calls, I should answer." I believe he was sorry, and that I could help him fix his life. I thought that maybe, just maybe, we could work through our issues and come out stronger on the other side.

Just as I was thinking that, my phone rang. It was Marco calling. My heart skipped a beat as I hesitated for a moment before answering.

"Hey Marco," I said, trying to sound calm despite the fear in my voice.

"Baby listen please...don't hang up," he said, his voice sounding desperate. "I'm really am sorry. I don't know what my mind was thinking about, I would never hurt you."

I took a deep breath and tried to process what he was saying. A part of me wanted to believe him, wanted to think that he was genuinely sorry and that we could move forward from here.

But another part of me was still hurt and angry. Remembering the way he had slapped me across the room.

Marco must have sensed my hesitation because he kept talking, trying to convince me to give him another chance.

"Can we try this again?" he asked. "Can I come over and talk to you?"

And like a dumb ass, I said yes.

In my mind, I'm thinking, "Lyric, what the hell is you thinking? My heart was telling me I still had feelings for him, and maybe- just maybe- we can work this shit out. These butterflies in my stomach got me nervous as fuck.

"Ok, sayless I'm on the way," Marco said.

I went into the living room, still sipping on my glass of champagne, waiting for Marco to arrive. My nerves were on edge, unsure of what to expect, but then there was a knock on the door, I knew it was him.

I got up to let him in, and we headed to the sofa to talk. Marco started off by saying, "Baby can I explain something to you?" He said, as he stared at me deep down in my soul, "I'm sorry about all the mess you went through with Keke at the mall, but that shit with Karmen was because she hated you."

I looked at him like he was crazy, "Why should I believe you?" Marco pulled out his phone and showed me some texts between him and Karmen. It seemed like Karmen had been talking to one of Marco's friends and was asking him when he was going to tell that other girl it was over.

"Bae, she tried to make it seem like I was messing around with her because she wanted a guy like me in her life," He said calmly. "Baby I would never mess with anybody like Karmen, I heard she for the streets anyway.”

Marco kept telling me that Karmen had been hating on me from the start, and she made it seem like he was cheating on me, when really she was just trying to 'cause drama. I dropped my head, feeling like a fool believing Karmen's lies.

Marco looked at me again and said, “Baby serious, I'm sorry. I will do anything to get you back in my life. I will never put my hands on you again.”

He sounded so serious that I believed every word he said. I told him that I was scared that he would hurt me again, but he promised me that he wouldn't. He said he loved me and wanted to be with me forever.

But then I asked him about Keke.

“What about the baby?” I asked.

He looked at me like it wasn't no big deal and said, “I ain't gonna disown my child, I will be there for him.” He responded.

I could not believe what I was hearing, A man that is willing to take care of his child. I wish my dad would have done that for me. Marco made me fall deeply in love with him after hearing that.

Marco must have sensed the way I was feeling about him because he started kissing

my neck and making me feel all kinds of good.
Then he laid me back on the sofa and started
kissing me all down my body, he opened my
legs and started eating my pussy... crazy style.
He tongue licked my clit in circular motions.

"I love this shit" he whispered as his
fingers slid inside my pussy, in and out,

"Mmm," He groaned loud and deep.

"You taste so good, Lyric," his hot breath
hit my spot. Then Marco grabbed my legs and
threw them over his shoulder and buried his
face deeper. His tongue vibrated against my
g-spot.

"Ahhh," I screamed loudly as the room
spun around us.

As Marco continued to eat my pussy, I
could feel the tension building up inside me.
His tongue was like a magic wand, teasing and
tantalizing my sensitive spots. I was getting
closer and closer to cummin', and I could feel
my body starting to shake.

"Ahahah." I moaned, my voice trembling
with pleasure. Marco's tongue moved faster
and faster, his lips sucking on my clit like a
vacuum. I felt like I was going to explode, and
then suddenly, I did.

My body convulsed in a wave of
pleasure, my pussy contracting and releasing in
a series of intense spasms. Marco kept eating

me out, his tongue licking up my juices as I came.

I scream loudly, my voice echoing through the room as I ride the wave of pleasure. Marco didn't stop until I was finished cumming, his tongue finally slowing down as he looked at me with a satisfied grin on his face.

"Damn, baby girl," he said, his voice husky with desire, "You taste so good."

I laid there, panting and trembling with pleasure, feeling like I had just been blown away by a hurricane. Marco had eaten my pussy like a pro, making me cum harder than I ever had before.

As I caught my breath, Marco leaned forward and kissed me softly on the lips. "I'm glad you enjoyed that," he whispered.

I nodded silently and that's when he told me, "I didn't wanna fuck you tonight, I just wanted to please you," he said.

I looked at him and asked him, "Why?"

He just smiled at me and said, "Cuz baby you deserve it." Then before you knew it me and Marco were knocked out on the sofa. Was he really trying to show me that he wants to change... I hope so.

Chapter 6

My alarm on my phone went off, blasting in my ear and making me jump. I reached over and turned it off, rubbing my eyes and trying to wake up. I looked around the room, seeing that Marco was nowhere to be found.

I got up off the sofa and started getting myself ready for the day, wondering where Marco was and what he was doing. That's when I saw a note on the kitchen table, with a plate full of breakfast food next to it.

I walked over to the table and picked up the note, reading it.

"Hey baby, I had to run out and take care of some things. I didn't want to wake you up, you was sleeping so peacefully. I made you some breakfast, hope you like it. I'll be back later, can't wait to see you again. Love Marco"

I smiled as I read the note, feeling a little touched by his thoughtfulness. Then I looked at the plate he made me for breakfast - scrambled eggs with cheese, bacon, and french toast.

"Damn, dis nigga can cook," I said to myself.

I sat down at the table and started eating, savoring the taste of the food. It was good...real good. As I ate, my phone started ringing. It was Marco.

"Hey baby," he said "I'm on the way back to you."

"Hey," I replied. "What you doing today?"

"I'm taking you shopping today," he said. "We need to get some new clothes for you and some other things."

"Cool...what time you coming to pick me up?" I asked.

"In about an hour, get sexy for me," he said, his voice low and seductive.

My heart skipped a beat as I heard him say that.

"Okay daddy," I said while hanging up the phone.

I finished getting ready, throwing on a fire outfit that consisted of a tight black dress that hugged my curves in all the right places, and some cute ass Gucci sandals that made my toes look all pretty and whatnot. My hair was done up in a sleek ponytail, and my makeup was flawless - with my lip gloss popping and some dramatic eyelashes. I was feeling like a boss, and I couldn't wait to see my man.

As I finished up, I heard a knock at the door. I knew it was Marco, so I grabbed my purse and headed to the door. I opened it up, and there he was, looking sexy as fuck. He was rocking a black shirt that showed off his muscles, and some fitted jeans that accentuated his assets. His hair was cut, nice fade with the waves, oh yes, they were spinning.

"What's good, baby?" he asked, smiling at me all sly-like.

"Ain't nothing daddy," I replied, smiling back at him all seductive-like.

He walked in and gave me a kiss on the cheek. "Damn baby you look good," he said.

"Thanks daddy," I said, feeling all flattered and shit.

We stood there for a minute, just vibing with each other's energy. Then Marco spoke up again.

"Let's get going, we got some shopping to do."

"Aight bet," I said, grabbing my keys out of my purse and locking the door behind me. As we walked to the car, Marco had his arm around me. He smelled good as fuck.

"You smell good daddy." I said to him as we got in the car.

"Thanks ma" he replied as he started up the engine, and then we pulled off.

As we pulled out the driveway, Marco's phone started ringing. He looked at the screen and sighed, clearly annoyed.

"Who is it?" I asked, curious.

"It's Keke," he replied, his voice firm.

I raised an eyebrow, wondering what she wanted. Marco answered the phone, and I could hear Keke's voice on the other end, sounding all dramatic and shit.

"Marco, I need to talk to you about us," she said.

Marco sighed again, clearly impatient.

"Keke, I told you before. I'm with my girl now. I don't have time for your games."

Keke started talking again, but Marco cut her off. "Listen, Keke. I'm in the car with my girl right now. You don't need to be contacting me until the baby is born. And even then, It's just about the baby. You feel me?"

I could hear Keke's voice getting all loud and angry on the other end of the line, but Marco just kept it real with her.

"I mean it, Keke. Don't call me again unless it's about the baby. And don't even think about showing up at my crib unannounced. You got that?"

Keke must have gotten the message loud and clear because she didn't say nothing else after that.

"Aight," Marco said finally before hanging up the phone.

He looked over at me and smiled, "Sorry bout that."

I shook my head. "Ain't nothing to be sorry bout."

As we pulled up at the mall, I was hyped, ain't gonna lie. Marco right by my side is all I needed. We got out of the car and started walking towards the entrance, our arms all entwined like lovers on a mission.

The mall was jumping, people was everywhere, but we navigated through the crowds like we owned the place. Marco spotted this store he liked and veered off towards it, his hands still collapsed around mine. I followed him in, taking in the sights and sounds of the bustling retail space. The air was thick with the smell of fresh clothes and perfumes, and I felt like a kid in a candy store as we started browsing through the racks.

Marco started trying on new fits, looking all good and stuff. He came out of the dressing room modeling the clothes, this man knew he was fine. I couldn't help but laugh at his antics, feeling carefree and alive for the first time in weeks. That's when I saw this dude walking towards us - Kwame, my old friend from high school.

"Kwame!" I exclaimed, surprised by his sudden appearance. We hugged each other tight, exchanging new things that have happened in our lives since high school. Marco watched us with an unreadable expression on his face before finally intervening with a curt "Wassup" directed at Kwame. Kwame threw his head up at Marco.

I could tell that Marco was getting aggy or something, but I ain't think nothing of it at first. Me and Kwame kept catching up for a hot second before Marco finally spoke, "I'ma go to the bathroom real quick." I nodded and kept talking to Kwame.

I was not worried about any drama today. I was so glad to be out of the house with Marco and catching up on good times with Kwame. I was at peace today and I was happy.

But then Marco came back, and something was off. His eyes looked all glassy, and his whole attitude had changed. He was walking all slow and deliberate, like he was in a trance or something.

"Marco, you okay?" I asked, noticing that he seemed a little...off.

But he just shook his head and kept staring at me. All of a sudden, he grabbed my arm tight and said "I'm ready to go!"

I was shocked by his sudden change in behavior. "What's wrong?" I asked, trying to pull my arm away from him.

But Marco just tightened his grip. "I'm tired of you embarrassing me," he said, his voice low and menacing. "Why you acting like a slut in public, flirting with other niggas and shit. I'm tired of it."

I felt a surge of anger at his words. "What are you talking about?" I demanded. " I wasn't doing nothing, just catching up with an old friend."

Kwame looked at us with concern etched on his face when Marco was talking to me.

"Brah, why you grabbing her like that?"Kwame said.

"Yo, you need to stay outta this one. This ain't got nothing to do with you." Marco responded.

Kwame nodded and backed away slowly.

"I didn't mean to cause no problems, lyric," said Kwame.

"It's cool Kwame," I replied.

"I'll talk to you later,"he said.

Kwame then walked off leaving me alone. Marco started pulling me towards the exit.

"Let's go," he growled.

As we walked out of the mall together is when everything went bad to worse. We were walking to the car, Marco was still going off on me, talking all kinds of shit.

"You always doing this, Lyric," he said, his voice low and menacing. "You always flirting with other niggas, thinking you can just get away with it."

I was getting tired of his accusations, and I could feel my anger rising up. "Marco, I ain't doing nothing," I said, trying to keep my cool.

But he just kept going, his words cutting deep. "You just a hoe, Lyric." he said. "You'll fuck any nigga that looks at you."

We were walking side by side, but Marco's anger was palpable. He was getting more and more agitated by the second.

"Did you fuck that nigga?" he asked suddenly, his eyes narrowed.

I stopped dead in my tracks, shocked by the question. "What? No, Marco," I said. "We went to school together, that's all."

But Marco didn't believe me. He just laughed and said, "Save it, Lyric. You ain't shit but a hoe." He didn't give a damn what he said to me at this moment. He cut me deep in my soul.

"You think you the shit, walking around letting niggas hug you and shit," he spat at me. "But you ain't nothing. You're just a piece of ass to me."

I felt tears prickling at the corners of my eyes as Marco's words washed over me like a wave of pain.

"You're nothing, Lyric." he repeated again and again when I finally had enough.

"What the fuck is your problem?" I demanded.

That's when Marco turned around and slapped the shit out of me. My head snapped back from the force of the slap and I hit the ground. I know this shit ain't happen again.

As I sat on the ground, stunned from the slap, Marco stood over me, his eyes blazing with anger. The intensity of his gaze made my skin crawl, and I could feel my heart racing with fear and anticipation. The sound of my own ragged breathing filled my ears, and I felt like I was trapped in a nightmare from which I couldn't wake up.

"Get up, bitch," Marco said to me, his voice dripping with venom.

The words hurt me so bad, and I felt a surge of anger mixed with fear. I slowly got to my feet, my eyes locked on Marco's as I tried to process what was happening. My mind was racing with thoughts of how to get out of this situation alive. "Why did you think he was going to change, Lyric?" I said to myself.

Marco's face was twisted in a snarl, his eyes narrowed into slits. He looked like a man possessed, and I knew I had to be careful.

"We'll finish this shit when we get home," he growled, his voice low and scary. The threat hung in the air like a challenge, and I knew I had to be prepared for what was coming.

He grabbed my arm pulling me towards the car, damn near dragging me along. I stumbled as he pulled, trying to keep up with him. The silence between us was oppressive, punctuated only by the sound of our footsteps on the pavement. My heart was pounding in my chest like a drum, and I felt like I was trapped in a never-ending cycle of fear.

As we reached the car, Marco finally said something, "You think you can disrespect me like that? He said, "I'ma show you what happens when you cross me."

I was scared and didn't know if I was going to die today. Marco's anger radiated off him like heat from a fire. I knew I had to tread carefully If I wanted to get out of this situation. The air seemed to vibrate with tension as Marco's anger hung in the balance. I felt trapped and alone with no way out.

As we reached the house, Marco turned off the engine and turned to me.

"Get your ass in the muthafuckin' house right now," he said. His eyes squinted up and his eyebrow raised.

He got out of the car, slammed the door while watching me walk to the door. We walked in the house in silence which seemed ever more ominous than if he had been yelling and screaming at the top of his lungs. As soon as we stepped inside when I felt the chill run down my spine, I didn't know what Marco was going to do to me.

"You Bitch! You think you're going to go out here and do shit like that in front of me?" he asked. "So now bitch I'ma show you the real me now."

My heart sank as I realized that Marco's anger had finally reached its boiling point. There was no turning back now, no escape from the abuse that I was about to go through. There was no way out this time.

Chapter 7

As I stood there, frozen in fear, Marco's words made me feel like I had died and went to hell. Like someone had cut me with a sharp razor knife straight in my heart. I felt like the walls were closing in on me, I couldn't feel anything. I was so numb and I could feel my heart pounding real hard.

"You're a stupid bitch," Marco said to me, his voice all rough and gravelly like he'd been smoking cigarettes all day. "You will do what I say here on out or you'll die, take your pick?" he yelled at me, his eyes blazing with fury. "You're mine now!"

I felt so many mixed emotions going on in my head as Marco was talking to me. I knew I had to be careful now and watch what I say. But as I looked into his eyes, I saw something that made my blood run cold. It was a look of pure hate, a look that said he didn't care if he hurt me or not.

He took a step closer to me, his fist clenched at his sides. "From here on out," he said to me, "You don't leave this house unless I say so." His voice was very low and I can tell he meant business.

I tried to speak up for myself but my voice came out all shaky and weak, "B-but what about my job at the club?"

Marco laughed right IN MY FACE... "That's a dub," he said with a sneer. "You belong to me now, ain't nobody else getting their hands on you." He took another step closer to me, his eyes gleaming with excitement.

"And if you ever try to leave me or cross me again... I'll make sure it's your last time," he said as he mushed me in my face.

All I could do was cry. The man who had made passionate love to me, who whispered sweet nothings in my ear, was a monster... And I had no idea. There were no red flags, no warning signs or anything when I met this man. He had hidden his true self behind a mask of charm and charisma, and I had fallen for it. I was like a fish that caught the wrong hook line, pulled out and gutted.

I just stood there in silence, I couldn't move, I was stuck, that's when Marco got a phone call.

"I'll be back," he said curtly as he gave me a look that sent shivers down my spine...

"Bitch and I want you to try to leave," as he left and slammed the door behind him.

I couldn't feel my body; I was numb all over like I had just been hypnotized.

I walked to the room in a daze, grabbing my pillow like it was the only thing that could comfort me now. I laid across the bed hugging that pillow tight and trying to hold back tears but they just kept flowing. All I could think about is how did I end up here? How did I let this happen? Why didn't I see right through his lies?

The more I thought about it, the more the tears just kept coming... My heart felt like it had broken into pieces and was never going to be whole again. I just kept laying there, my body shaking like a leaf, my face is throbbing in pain from when Marco hit me. I was scared, so scared, that I couldn't even fight any more. I was just so tired, so fed up and hurt, I cried myself straight to sleep.

Time had flown by so fast and before I knew it, morning had broken, but Marco was still nowhere to be found. Same ol' bullshit, different day.

I reached over to my nightstand and grabbed my phone, and that's when I saw all the missed calls from Marco. The fuck? I was knocked out cold and didn't hear shit. Even

Passion had called me, but I didn't have time to think about what she wanted right now. I had to forget about Passion and call Marco back, ASAP. I dialed his number, my heart racing real fast.

"Bitch, I'm bout to pull up," he said, his voice cold and he didn't care, and then he hung up on me.

"Here we go again," I said to myself.

I know Marco must've been speeding because someone was banging on the door like they were trying to break it down. And I knew it was him.

I opened the door and I tried to walk away but Marco stopped me dead in my tracks.

"Come here," he said.

I turned around to see what he wanted, he grabbed me by my neck like he was trying to choke the life out of me. He pulled me close to him, stuck his fingers in my panties...

And then he felt my pussy... he felt that I was wet. He looked at me with a mixture of anger and lust in his eyes.

"This is why you couldn't answer your phone?" he sneered at me. Marco grabbed me harder and punched me right in my face. There I went again...Back on the floor. My head spinning, my vision blurry. Lord, what did I do to deserve this?

"Get up," Marco yelled at me, His voice echoing off the walls. "You got work to do."

I slowly got to my feet, my body aching all over. I looked up at him, my eyes filled with tears and pain.

"What is it that you need me to do?" I asked him, my voice shaking.

"I'm having a party tonight," he said. "And you're gonna cook for all my guests."

I felt a cool breeze of fear run through me. I didn't want to cook for his friends. I didn't want to be around them. But Marco didn't care about what I wanted. He just cared about what he wanted.

"Get to work," he said. "Clean the house from top to bottom. Cook enough food for 20 people. And make sure you look good doing it."

I nodded slowly as Marco handed me a list of things to do.

"Don't forget nothing," he said. "I'll be watching you."

I started cleaning the house, even though I didn't feel like it. I swept and mopped the floors, wiped down the counters, and cleaned the bathrooms. I had done everything he had asked me to do on his list. I had to make sure that I didn't forget nothing.

As I worked, I couldn't help but think about how much I hated this life. I hated being trapped in this situation with no kind of support or hardly no one to call on, afraid that he would find out and kill me. I hated being treated like I'm a slave forced to do Marco's bidding without any say in the matter.

But most of all, I hated Marco. I hated him for what he has done to me, for what he continued to do to me. I hated him for taking away my freedom, for taking away my dignity.

As I finished up the cleaning, Marco came into the kitchen. He opened up the fridge and handed me some bags with food in them.

"Good, you finished cleaning," he said. "Now start cooking. I got a lot of people coming over tonight, so make this shit look perfect."

I started cooking the food like Marco said, trying to make sure everything was the way he wanted it. I seasoned the ground beef and started fixing the cheeseburger casserole. I put the steaks on the grill and started cooking them. I cut up the collards and put them in the pot to let them cook slowly.

As I cooked, Marco walked around the kitchen, checking on everything. He tasted the food and made suggestions for how to make it better. Everything had to be his way, and I was not about to argue with him.

"You need to add more salt to this," he said, tasting the cheeseburger casserole. "And you need to flip them steaks over," he said, looking at the grill.

I nodded and made the adjustments, trying not to piss him off. Marco had turned me into someone that was scared to even fart loud around him. His whole vibe changed from being my prince charming, and now he is just someone I regret meeting.

As the food started to come together, Marco's friends began to arrive. They came into the kitchen, smelling the food and complimenting me on the cooking.

"Damn, this smells good," one of them said.

"Shorty, you be putting in work in the kitchen," another one said.

I smiled and thanked them and then I looked up, Marco's expression changed in an instant. He came over to the kitchen, his eyes narrowing at me.

"What's going on here?" he asked, with a smirk.

I felt my hands getting sweaty, I knew something was about to happen. I knew how jealous Marco got, but I know damn well he didn't think I would do that to his friends. I was just being polite trying to make his party go well.

"Nothing, Marco," I said quickly. "Just responding to your friends."

But Marco was not feeling that shit. He looked at me like I was doing something wrong. Everything I did in his eyes was wrong.

"Looks like the food is almost done," he said. "I can watch it the rest of the time. You can go in the other room until I'm done with my homies."

I felt really bad, like why did I have to leave the party and not be able to attend. He threw a party in my apartment and I'm not even allowed to attend. I just don't understand this man at all.

"Damn, that's cold," I said to myself in my head."

I looked at Marco, but he just turned his back on me and started tending to the food. I knew better than to argue with him, so I just nodded and walked away.

As I left the kitchen, I could feel the eyes of Marco's friends on me. They seemed to sense the tension between us, but they didn't say anything.

I walked in the other room and sat down on the couch, feeling like a prisoner in my own home. Why couldn't Marco just let me be? Why did he always have to control everything"?

I sat there for what felt like hours, listening to the sounds of laughter and music coming from the other room. It was like I was invisible, like I didn't exist. And that feeling hurt more than anything else. I felt so isolated in my own house.

Just as I was drifting off into my own thoughts, one of Marco's homeboys came into the living room where I was. He was a tall, light skinned dude with dreads hanging past his shoulders. I turned my nose up because why the fuck was he in here and everyone else in the kitchen.

"What's good, Lyric?" he asked, sitting down next to me on the couch.

I looked at him, trying to be polite. "Not much, just chillin'," I replied.

He nodded and looked around the room. "This is a nice home you got here.Marco did well for himself," he said.

I smiled weakly, not knowing what to say.

But before I could respond, Marco's homeboy started talking again.

"So Lyric, what do you like to do for fun?" he asked.

I shrugged, trying to play it cool. "I don't know, just hang out with my homegirls and family, I guess."

He nodded and kept talking, asking me questions about myself and listening intently to my responses. But as we talked, I could feel Marco's eyes on us from across the room. I knew he was getting jealous, and I didn"t want any trouble.

Then all of a sudden Marco's friend said something that made me laugh...

"Man, my girl can't decorate to save her life," he said. "Our house look a hot mess...swear to god."

I giggled at his joke...

But then Marco stormed into the living room...

"What do we have here?" he asked rudely. "Shit I wanna laugh too... Let me get on the conversation."

Marco's homeboy stood up quickly, "Damn Marco man calm down." He said. " I told her about how my girl can't decorate. Our house is all fucked up right now," he laughed.

Marco glared at his friend, "You think that shit funny?"

His homeboy shook his head quickly, "Nah man it aint nothing like that," He explained.

But Marco was not feeling none of that. "You need to leave her alone," he said in a rude way.

As the tension between them grew thicker, Marco turned toward me and just gave me that look. That look that gave me the feeling he wanted to take my head off right now.

"So you thought the shit he was saying was funny huh?" he shouted with anger. His face was red with rage and his eyes was glassy as fuck. I know I had to think carefully about how to answer him. The vibe in the room had shifted dramatically as Marco yelled out to his homies in the kitchen.

"Yo, everybody come check this out! We have a situation here!" he said laughing.

The sound of footsteps filled the air as they all gathered around us. The air was so thick with anticipation and hostility as they all wanted something to go down. My heart sank as I realized that I had got myself in some more shit. I had the feeling that this was about to be a long night for me. "Why the fuck did he call all his homies in the living for?" I said to myself. This shit is unreal.

Chapter 8

I could not believe what was happening. Marco was standing there, talking to his homies like I was some kinda piece of property. "Now, y'all finally get to meet the famous Lyric, " he said, smiling like he was the king of the city. "She was one of the easy ones, just a lil side bitch looking for a good time."

His homies all started laughing and nodding in agreement. I felt my face heat up with shame and anger. How could he do this to me?

"And since she wanna sit here and talk to my homie." Marco continued, his voice dripping with malice, "let's do this right here. Lyric, show them how you can suck a mean dick."

I couldn't believe what I was hearing. Was he serious? Did he really think I would do something like that in front of all these people?

All his homies started getting hyped, like they were waiting for a show or something. They didn't care about me or my feelings, all they cared about was seeing what Marco was talking about.

I looked up at Marco, trying to plead with him to stop this nonsense.

"What Marco, not in front of them," I said, trying to keep my voice low."

But Marco just gave me that look, that look that said "Bitch, if you don't do what I say, I'll kill you tonight." I knew he wasn't playing, so I did what he said.

I dropped down to my knees, unbuckled his belt and pulled his dick out. His homies all started cheering and chanting, like they were at some kinda sick perverted parade. As I started sucking, all his homies pulled out their phones and started recording. They didn't care about me or my dignity, no more than Marco did.

The humiliation burned inside me like a fire as the tears streamed down my face while sucking Marco's nasty ass hard dick. He got his hands in my hair, pulling my head back and forth, trying to show out and take control. His homies are closing in around us, their faces all twisted up like they were enjoying this shit.

One of them grabbed my titty and squeezed it hard as hell, making me wince in pain. Another one slapped my ass so hard it made me jump. I feel like I'm about to lose it, like I'm stuck in some never-ending nightmare.

Then Marco pulled it outta my mouth and grabbed my chin, making me look at him.

His eyes are cold as ice, his voice all menacing and shit as he says, "You ain't done yet, bitch. You're gonna finish what you started.

Now, I'm finally get up off my knees, sitting on the couch, feeling like I just hit rock bottom. I just finished sucking Marco off in front of his sick friends. I felt so embarrassed and humiliated. Marco came over and stood right next to me and grabbed me by my hair and pulled my head back.

I closed my eyes, trying to avoid contact with him. His boys still watching us like they at a fucking Superbowl party, staring at me like I'm some kind of freak. I just want to disappear.

Marco started laughing, talking trash to his boys about how I just sucked his dick and he can make me do whatever he says. I felt like a dog that was being trained.

And then he said the unthinkable: "Y'all want a piece of this?" he nodded toward me, offering me up to his boys like I was a prostitute on the corner. I feel a wave of shame and disgust wash over me as Marco said those words. I'm trying to process what's going on, but it's like my mind just went blank. I'm trapped in the devil's castle and can't leave.

Marco's homies are looking at me with a mix of lust and curiosity, and I can tell they're considering Marco's offer. One of them takes a step forward, his eyes locked on me with a hungry gaze.

"Y-yes," he says, his voice low and rough. "I'll take some."

My heart sinks as Marco nods, smiling like he's proud of him. He steps aside letting his boy take his place.

"No," I whispered, trying to push him away. But he's too strong , too powerful. He grabs my arms, holding me down as he starts to undo his pants. I'm feeling like I'm gonna pass out from the fear and the shame. This can't be happening! I can't do nothing about it, this man is too powerful for me.

The room starts to spin around me as the boy starts to touch me, his hands roaming over my body like I'm some kind of object. I feel like I'm losing myself, losing my grip on reality. And then there are more hands on me, more bodies closing in around me. Marco's boys are taking turns with me, using me for their own sick pleasure.

I'm trapped in this hellhole, surrounded by monsters who don't care about feelings or well-being. They just want to use me to get a nut.

As the night wears on, things get more intense, more chaotic. The music is loud, the laughter is loud, big smoke clouds everywhere, and all I can do is just lay there frozen.

As the last niggas finishes with me, I'm left laying on the couch, feeling like I've been fucked in every way possible. My body's sore, my mind racing, and I just wanna leave this house and never look back.

But before I can even process what just went down, Marco comes over to me, looking at me like I was dirty.

"Clean yo'self up, bitch," he says, his voice all rude. "And then clean this muthafuckin' house. Me and my niggas is going out, and this shit better be spotless when I get back."

I'm sitting there thinking, "Why this nigga talkin' to me like that? This ain't even his crib." But all I can do is nod my head and do what he said, cause I know If I don't, he'll flip out on me.

I slowly get up from the couch, my legs shaking like a leaf. I make my way to the bathroom, trying to hold back tears as I look at myself in the mirror. My eyes all swollen, my face is still bruised up, and my body is covered in all kinds of liquids from them niggas.

I took a deep breath and started cleaning myself up. The shower water stings like a muthafucka as it hits my skin, but It's a welcome relief from the pain. As I'm cleaning, I keep thinking about how Marco's treating me like I am one of his slaves. He don't give a fuck about how I feel or what just happened - all he care about is getting what he want.

After what feels like an eternity in the bathroom, I came out. Now it's time for part two of Marco's order - clean this whole muthafuckin house, Its beer bottles every, so it's gonna take some time, and I know I gotta make sure it's spotless or Marco is going to have a fit.

I stepped into the kitchen, feeling like a brand new woman. The shower water has washed away most of the pain, but the emotional scars still lingered. I took a deep breath, and got to work on cleaning the house. Marco's orders echoed in my mind - clean this whole muthafuckin house, make sure it's spotless.

I put on some music, something to take my mind off of things. I started vacuuming, twerking to the beat as I glided across the floor. The music was loud, but it wasn't loud enough to drown out the thoughts of Marco and his abuse.

As I cleaned, I felt myself getting into a zone. The vacuum was my dance partner, and we were killing it. I spun and twirled, and really was enjoying myself. It felt like it was nobody on earth but me and I was free to do whatever I wanted.

The house was almost clean, and I was feeling like I had cleaned everything from top to bottom. With music in your ear and you zone yourself out, time goes by so fast. That's when my phone rang, interrupting the whole vibe.

It was Marco, I answered it in a rush thinking he was checking in on me. But it wasn't him. It was his friend...the one who had been talking to me in the living room earlier.

"Yo, lyric," he said.

I didn't say anything, just waiting for him to spit out whatever he had to say. I had felt like it was a set up, so I was very nervous to even speak.

"Marco's high right now," he said. "He done tried to fight every nigga that crossed his path tonight."

My heart sank as I realized what this meant.

"He's probably gonna try to hit on you when he gets home," his friend warned me. "I just want to give you a heads up."

I stood there frozen. All I could say was "I gotta go" before hanging up the phone. Then reality set in, Marco was coming home and he was gonna be angry...and hurtful...and abusive.

I needed something to numb myself. Something to take away the pain and take my mind off the abuse.

So I walked over to the cabinet and grabbed some Vodka.Then I went into my room and grabbed my stash - a pink container that I used to hold my jewelry but now it held something much more valuable...Cocaine.

I sat there, sipping on vodka, feeling the burn as it went down my throat. Then I did a few lines of cocaine, feeling the rush as it hit my system. I was in a zone, numb to everything around me.

It felt like I was on stage again, with thousands of fans screaming my name. I was in the spotlight, and nothing else mattered. The music was pumping, and I was dancing all around the living room.

But then, suddenly, I heard a car pull up outside. The music was loud, and the door slammed shut. I didn't even flinch, too numb to care. Forgot Marco had took my keys, he used them to open the door and walked in looking like the devil himself. He slammed the door behind him, and I just sat there, staring at him.

"Hey, how was your night?" I asked him, my voice slurred to the vodka.

Marco walked over to me with a smirk on his face and stared at me. He grabbed me and punched me dead in my face, over and over again. I felt like he was trying to kill me.

Then he grabbed me by my shirt and smacked me again. I fell onto the other couch, and turned over and couldn't move. Marco rushed over to me and started choking me so hard, I couldn't catch my breath. The stronger he put pressure on my neck, the more air I was gasping for. It was like something had come over him, possessing his body.

But then all of a sudden, he let me go and started crying. I'm coughing trying to catch my breath, blood dripping from my face and all I could do is just look at him.

I'm shaking, but numb all over. Why was I still sitting here? My dumb ass was so in love, I grabbed him and just held his head. Too many   people warned me about Marco, But me...I was stuck on stupid. I just sat there with him until he fell asleep.

I got up slowly, my body aching from Marco beating me. I made my way to the bathroom, my legs were shaking like a leaf. I turned on the light, and the brightness made me squint.

I looked in the mirror, and my heart just started beating fast. My face was all fucked up, all brusied up and swollen. My eye was blacked and closed, like I had just got out of a boxing ring.

I couldn't believe it. I started crying, tears streaming down my face like rain. How did it come to this? How did I let Marco do this to me over and over again?

I looked at myself, and I didn't even recognize the person that was staring back at me. The girl in the mirror was broken, battered, and bruised. She was a shadow of her former self.

I cried some more, feeling sorry for myself. Why did I stay with him? Why did I let him do this to me?

I thought about all the times he had hurt me before. All the times he had punched me, kicked me and choked me. And now this.

I wiped away my tears and took a closer look at myself. My face was a mess, but it wasn't just physical damage that Marco had done to me. He had also damaged my soul.

I cleaned my face the best way I could, trying to wipe away the blood, but the rag and peroxide was burning. After doing that, I went back into the living room and laid down on the couch beside Marco. He was still asleep, oblivious to the pain he had caused.

As I looked at him, I thought to myself, "Fuck this shit, Lyric. Love don't hurt like that."

But why was I still here? Why was I still with him?

I knew I deserved better. I knew I shouldn't be treated like this. But somehow, I had convinced myself that this was love.

"Fuck that," I said to myself. "This ain't love, this is some bullshit."

But as I looked at Marco, seeing him sleep so peaceful, something inside me still felt for him. Maybe it was loyalty, maybe it was fear, or maybe it was just plain ol' stupidity.

Whatever it was, it kept me there beside him, even though everything in my body told me to get up and leave. As the tears dried on my face and the pain started to set in again.

Everyone thought I was stupid for staying with him. My friends, my family, they all said I deserved better. They all said Marco was a monster, and that I should leave him before he killed me.

My eyes hurt, but my eyelids were heavy. I was so tired and my body was so exhausted. And before I knew it I had fallen asleep right there with Marco. I knew I deserve better than this, I was just so scared to leave. It was like do as he says or be buried six feet under. I had so much on my mind, what did life have planned for me next? Or should I say what's next for me and Marco?

Chapter 9

The next morning, I woke up to an empty house. No Marco, he is up to his usually m.i.a shit as always. I got up off the couch, took a shower and got dressed. Then I went into the living room and sat down on the couch to watch some tv. I was chilling, trying to relax and forget about all the bullshit that went down last night.

Just as I'm getting into my show, my phone rings. It's Passion, my homegirl from work. "Lyric where have you been? She asks, her voice all high-pitched and concerned. "You ain't been to work or nothing. What's good?"

I had to think fast and come up with a lie. "I've been sick," I said, trying to sound convincing. "I think I caught somethin' from the club. I didn't wanna come back and infect nobody."

But Passion wasn't trying to hear that shit. "That's bullshit," she said bluntly. "You've been in here with cold chills and you still came to work? Rumors round town you letting Marco beat your ass like a punching bag."

I got quiet, didn't know what to say.

Passion kept going, her voice all rude and shit. "Girl, wtf? You need to leave his ass before he kills you. Ain't that much love in the world for nobody to be treating you like that."

I tried to defend Marco, "Girl it wasn't even like that." I explained. "He's just been going through things," I said quietly. "He didn't mean to do it.

But Passion cut me off, her voice rising in anger. "Okay, answer your facetime and let me see what he didn't mean to do." she said.

She rang me on Facetime, and I answered hesitantly. As soon as she saw my face on the screen...

"Lyric," she swore like I did something wrong. "Look at your damn face! You not a damn punching bag...girl! I will be there before I head into work. No excuses TF," and then she hung up.

Right as she hung up, guess who walked in? Marco, looking like he just won some kinda award, with a bouquet of roses.

"Hey baby," he said softly, holding out the roses. "I brought you something,"

I just stood there and looked at the roses. He always beats me and then he comes back with these sorry excuses. It be the look in his eyes that gets to me every time.

But before I could respond, the doorbell rings. It was Passion.

"I told you I was coming over," she said firmly, looking at Marco with her nose turned up.

"What's good Passion," Marco asked gruffly.

"Not shit," Passion replied curtly.

We stood there for a moment, just staring at each other. That's when passion opened her mouth and all hell broke loose

"You better check yourself Marco before I do," Passion says firmly, looking Marco dead in his eyes.

Marco takes a step back, looking all kinds of threatened.

"Or what?" he asks, trying to sound all tough.

Passion smiles sweetly, "Or I'll make sure everybody know what kind of nigga you is," she says.

Marco looks back at passion, "I ain't never laid a hand on her," he says.

Passion laughs loudly, "Oh really?" she says. Then why lyric got bruises all over her face?"

Marco looks at me then back at Passion, "I..." he starts but Passion cuts him off.

"Don't even try it," Passion says firmly.

Passion voice was like a razor, cutting deep and sharp. "You better get yo' self together, Lyric," she said. "You can't keep letting this nigga beat you like this. You deserve better than that."

I felt a surge of defensiveness, but before I could say anything, Marco spoke up.

"This my bitch," he said, his voice all possessive and controlling. "And she knows what's good for her."

Passion laughed, cold and mirthless sound. "Oh, so now you're talking huh?" she said. "You think you can come at me like that and I'll back down? Nah, nigga, I ain't going nowhere."

Marco steps forward, his eyes flashing with anger. "Mind yo' business, Passion," he said. "This ain't got nothing to do with you."

Passion snorted. "None of my business? You think I'm gonna stand by and watch you beat on my homegirl like she's some kinda of punching bag? Hell no, nigga. I got something to say about that."

The two of them went back and forth like that for a minute, their voices getting louder and more heated by the second.

Finally, Marco had enough. "Lyric,"he said, his voice cold and hard.

"Put this bitch out."

I hesitated for a second, unsure of what to do. But then I remembered all the times Marco had hurt me, all the times he'd made me feel small and worthless.

"Please leave Passion," I said finally, my voice firm. "Me and Marco have to work this out."

"Lyric, why is being so stupid? This man does not love you. When are you going to realize that?" Passion said.

"I will call you later, Passion," I mumbled.

Passion smiled sweaty at Marco before turning to leave. "This ain't over," she said over her shoulder. "And when she leaves your ass high and dry you gonna see how that shit feels." as she laughs and then slams the door.

Marco walked to the door and locked it after Passion left. Marco walked back to the living room, his face twisted with anger. "I don't want to see Passion over here no more," he said, his voice firm.

I nodded quickly, trying to avoid any more conflict. "Yes," I said.

Marco's expression softened slightly, and he took a step closer to me. "Baby, I'm sorry about last night," he said, his voice low and husky. "I really didn't mean it, and I promise you, it will never happen again.

I felt a lump in my throat as I looked up at him. "I'm scared," I whispered.

Marco's face contorted with emotion, and he pulled me into his arms. "Shh, baby," he whispered into my ear. "I love you, and I promise you, I will never hurt you again."

He whispered sweet nothings into my ear for a few minutes before pulling back and looking at me with them dreamy eyes.

"I got you somethin'," he said softly. To make it up to you, I went out this morning, got some roses.

He handed me the beautiful bouquet of red roses. He also got me this beautiful ass Dolce & Gabbana dress I have ever seen and the heels that match. I can't even lie, the shoes was sexy as fuck.

"Get dressed baby," Marco says, smiling so sweetly at me. We going out for lunch today. I was smiling from ear to ear, not knowing what was going on, but I loved it.

I went into the room and started to get dressed and do my makeup, trying to cover up the bruises on my face. Marco was waiting for me, looking all patient and whatnot. When I finally came to the living room, he was smiling really hard.

"Damn baby," he said, his voice all smooth and silky. "You look beautiful."

I blushed a little bit, feeling like a queen in my new dress and heels. Marco waited until I walked out first, watching me prissy walk out the door. And when I walked... I slayed.

We walked towards the car, and Marco opened the door for me like a gentleman. He showed me a whole different person today, one that was kind and gentle.

We got in the car and started listening to music, vibing together like we used to before all the drama started. Marco was holding my hand, stroking it gently with his fingers. And then he kissed it, making me feel all kinds of special.

Was this a changed man or what? Whatever it was, I was happy.

After driving for a little bit, we pulled into this fancy restaurant called "The Platinum Room". It was one of those high-end spots that only celebrities and rich folks go to.

Marco parked the car and came around to open the door for me again. He helped me out and we walked into the restaurant together, hand in hand.

The Platinum Room was even more beautiful than the outside. The decor was sleek and modern, with dim lighting and soft music playing in the background. We were greeted by the hostess who showed us to our table by the window.

As we sat down, Marco looked at me with his eyes. "I'm glad we could make it out for a night" he said softly. I smiled back at him, feeling like everything is gonna be alright.

"I'm glad too," I replied.

Then Marco raised his glass, "To new beginnings!" he said, as I raised my glass too, clinked it against his glass, "To new beginnings!" I said.

The moment was just so perfect. We were sitting at the table and just smiling back and forth. Marco started looking at me over the menu. He was talking to the waiter, ordering all kinds of fancy food.

"I'll have a lobster risotto meal," he said. And my girl will have the same." I nodded in agreement, feeling like nothing could stop us now. We got our drinks, and Marco started telling me about his childhood.

"Baby, I had a rough childhood," he said, his voice all serious and whatnot. "My pops was abusive, always beating my mom and me. I had to grow up fast, learn how to defend myself."

I listened intently, feeling sorry for him. "What happened? I asked.

Marco took a deep breath before continuing. "My pops was a drunk, always coming home late at night and starting fights with my mom. He would beat her up terribly, and I would just sit there and watch, feeling helpless.”

He paused for a minute, collecting his thoughts.

“One time, he beat my mom so bad that she had to go to the hospital. I was only 10 years old at the time, but it stuck with me forever.”

“What about your mom?” I asked.

Marco’s expression turned sad. “She died when I was 15,” he said. “She got sick from all the streets and abuse she suffered over da years.”

I reached out and took Marco’s hand, feeling sorry for him.

“I’m so sorry,” I said.

Marco looked at me with sad puppy eyes. “It’s okay,” he said softly. It made me who I am today. My dad ruined me and made me this person.”

We sat there in silence for a minute, just enjoying each other's company.Then our food came, we dug in, savoring every bite of that delicious lobster risotto meal.

But then something caught my attention. A text from Passion.

“Hey girl” it read. “What’s good?”

I looked up at Marco who was still talking away. I was trying to be discreet, but Marco caught me looking at my phone. He stopped talking and looked at me with a serious expression.

"Baby, when we at dinner, it's so disrespectful to be texting," he said, his voice firm but controlled. "Can you please put that away? Matter fact: who was that anyway?

I hesitated for a second before answering. "It's Passion," I said.

Marco's expression changed instantly. He looked at me with anger.

"Passion?" he repeated. "What she want? That bitch always causing drama."

I shrugged. "I don't know. She just sent me a text."

Marco's eyes narrowed. " What did she say? You better not be talking to her about our business."

I sighed. Feeling like I was in trouble already. "She just asked me what's up," I said.

Marco's face turned red with anger. "You need to stop talking to her," he said, his voice raised. "She's toxic and she's only bringing drama into our relationships. You need to focus on us, not on that hoe."

He slammed his fist on the table, making me jump.

"Bitch, you better listen to what I say,"he yelled. "How can I change for you if your friends all up in our business?" You're mine now, and you'll do as I say. You need to stop talking to her, or you gonna regret it."

The other people in the restaurant started to stare, but Marco didn't care. He just kept going on, his voice getting louder and louder.

"You think them bitches gonna have your back like I do, huh?" he sneered. "Nobody is going to treat you better than I can."

I felt a chill run down my spine as he spoke. This nigga was crazy. He went from being so loveable, and then the next minute he was snapping. Like he did a whole bipolar transformation in minutes.

As Marco's anger reached a boil, he suddenly stood up, his face red with rage. He baited for the waiter, calling him over with a curt gesture.

"Check, please," he barked, his voice dripping with hostility.

The waiter scurried over, handing him the check with a nervous smile. Marco snatched it from him, his eyes flashing with fury. He tossed some cash on the table, then turned to me and growled.

"Now let's go."

My heart sank as he grabbed my arm and pulled me out of the restaurant. Lord, I was sick to my stomach. Was it just fear that was making me feel this way, or was something else going on? I didn't know what to think or feel as Marco dragged me out of the restaurant. I guess we'll find out.

Chapter 10

I couldn't believe how fast things had taken a turn for the worse. One minute we were good, laughing and joking together, and the next Marco was speeding down the highway like a fucking maniac. I was getting more and more anxious by the second, my stomach churning with nausea.

"Marco, slow the fuck down," I said, trying to keep my voice calm. "I'm not feeling good. I think I'm gonna throw up."

But Marco just ignored me, turning the music up instead. I felt like I was gonna lose it, my head was spinning and my body was shaking. What was going on with me, this has never happened before.

Before I knew it, we were pulling into the apartment complex. Marco pulled into the parking space and turned off the engine. But he didn't get out of the car, instead, he looked at me with a cold expression.

"Get out og the car, bitch," he said, his voice firm.

I look back at him like he was crazy. "The Fuck" I thought to myself.

"Where you goin'? I thought we was spending time together." I asked.

Marco just smirked at me. "I'm going to check on Keke," he said. "She lost the baby."

I had a gut feeling about some shit, so I just stared at him, eyes all narrowed. "That bitch was never pregnant, was she?" I asked.

Marco's smirk grew wider, sneaky as fuck. "You right," he said. "She never was."

My heart sank as he continued to talk.

"Me and her just been fucking," he said nonchalantly.

I felt like I had been punched right in my stomach. That right there hurt more than anything.

"So get your dumb ass in the house like I said and lock the door," Marco ordered me. "I'll be back later."

With that, I got out of the car and Marco drove off. Left me standing there looking stupid as fuck. I felt like a damn fool believing this nigga.

"WHAT THE FUCK!!!," I screamed walking into my apartment.

I stumbled trying to keep myself together, my stomach churning with nausea. I kicked off my heels and headed to the room, but before I could even make it to the bed, I felt like I was gonna throw up. I ran to the bathroom, barely making it to the toilet before I let out a loud heave.

I felt like shit, my body shaking and my mind racing. What the fuck was going on? Was it the food from the restaurant? But then my mind went into shock mode.

What if I'm pregnant? I thought to myself, my heart sinking like a rock.

I flushed the toilet and stood up, looking at myself in the mirror. My face was still fucked up from the other night, but I didn't care about that right now. I remembered that I had a pregnancy test in the cabinet, and I knew I had to take it.

I grabbed the test and felt like I was about to have a whole panic attack. Knowing that I could be pregnant with this fool's baby was stressful as hell.

"God, I don't want to be stuck with a baby and this man," I said out loud, feeling like my world was crumbling down around me.

I opened the pregnancy test and pulled my panties down and pee'd in the cup that comes with the test. I wiped myself and flushed the toilet, my nerves were torn and I was so afraid of what the results could be. I stuck the test into the cup and just waited.

I looked in the mirror and just dropped my head. Five minutes have passed, and I took a look at the pregnancy test. It said positive.

"Omg bitch you pregnant" I said to myself. All I could do is break down. How could this happen to me? All these questions kept running through my head as I cried uncontrollably.

I walked out of the bathroom, feeling like I'd been hit by a truck. My body was numb all over again, and my mind was racing with thoughts of the pregnancy test. I sat down on my bed, holding my pillow tight, and turned on the tv to something funny. I just had to get my mind together, ya feel me?

But then my phone rang, and it was Marco. "Hello" I said, trying to sound calm.

"I'll be home in a minute, and I got somebody with me," he said rudely.

I wasn't even in the mood for Marco's mess, but I knew him, and I knew it was about to be some crazy shit. Minutes passed, and Marco finally got there. I heard him unlock the door.

"Lyric, where you at?" he said.

"I'm here in the room," I responded

He walked in the room, and guess who this nigga had with him? Keke. I was too sick to even argue.

"Marco, what the fuck is going on?" I said. "Me and Keke gonna chill here for a lil while," he said nonchalantly.

All I could do is shake my head. I got up to walk into the living room, but Marco grabbed my arm and stopped me.

"Where you headed?" he asked.

"I'm going in the living room, I'm not feeling good.," he said.

But Marco wasn't on that type of time. "Nahh, you gonna sit in this room and watch me fuck Keke," he said with a smirk on his face.

I couldn't believe this nigga. He already beats me, but now he thinks I'ma sit here and watch him fuck another bitch? He got me all the way fucked up.

"I ain't watching ya'll do that shit," I said firmly.

Marco grabbed me by the throat and said, "Yes the fuck you is."

That's when I told him, "Go ahead...hit me. You gonna kill your baby if you do...that's right, I'm pregnant."

His face looked so shocked when I said that, but he still ain't give a fuck.

"You pregnant?" he asked, looking at me like a predator.

"Yes, I'm pregnant," I replied. "I just took a test."

He rubbed my belly, showing excitement.

"That's a good thang...Ima have a lil mini-me running around here," he showed a happy expression...but then his face changed.

"That's even better...don't need to fuck you no more..." he started to laugh maniacally. "So sit yo ass down...and watch me fuck this bitch."

I sat there, frozen in disgust, as Marco started to kiss all over Keke's body. He was sucking on her neck, her breast, and her lips, just like a dog ass nigga. Keke was moaning and groaning, enjoying every minute of it.

"Watch closely, Lyric," Marco said, his voice dripping with sadism. "I want you to see how a real woman gets fucked."

I felt like I was gonna throw up, but my body was paralyzed with shock and humiliation. Marco started to undress Keke, revealing her naked body to me. He was kissing and licking every inch of her skin, making me feel like I was gonna lose my mind.

Keke was spreading her legs wide open, inviting Marco to come inside her. He didn't waste no time, plunging his dick deep into her pussy. They were fucking like animals, grunting and groaning, while I sat there watching, feeling like a piece of shit.

Marco started to talk dirty to Keke, telling her how good her pussy was to him. He was calling her all kinds of nasty names, like "bitch" and "whore," while he pumped his dick in and out of her.

"I'ma cum in your mouth," Marco said, looking at Keke with a wicked grin.

Keke opened her mouth wide, ready to receive Marco's cum.

He pulled out his dick, jerked it off for a few seconds...then sprayed his cum all over Keke's face. She licked it up with glee, while I just sat there, watching ...feeling so humiliated. Like what the fuck is this nigga doing to me?

As I sat there, tears streaming down my face, Marco looked at me with a mixture of confusion and anger. "What the fuck you crying for now? He asked, his voice laced with sarcasm.

I just shook my head, unable to speak. I was pregnant with this man's baby, and he was doing me like this? It was too much to handle.

Marco started to laugh, a cold, mirthless sound. "Girl you pregnant, so I ain't gonna fuck you," he said. "But I'ma make your ass look bad as fuck."

Keke had the nerve to chime in, her voice dripping with malice. "Yea bitch, you knew what it was."

Marco told her to shut the fuck up, but not before she gave me a sly smile. Like she thought she had won or something. That girl was all action when Marco was around but at the mall she was on hush.

As they prepared to leave, Marco turned to Keke and said, "Let's go baby." He smacked her ass, and she giggled like a schoolgirl.

I just sat there, speechless. This nigga had me feeling like nothing, like I was just a piece of trash he could use and discard. I mean all the shit he has put me through and then he brings this bitch...to my house.

As they walked out the door, Marco turned back to me and said, "I'm finna go, I'll be back for dinner. You better make sure you cook something I like. I was like damn he must think I was a personal chef or something. I just nodded, still trying to process everything that had just happened.

The door closed behind them, and I was left sitting there, alone with my thoughts. Pregnant with this man's baby, and he's out here doing me dirty with another bitch. I didn't know how much more of this shit I could take. But one thing was for sure - something had to give.

I got up out the chair, still feeling like shit, but I knew I had to get my mind right, and cooking for Marco was the last thing on my mind. But I didn't wanna hear his mouth, so I started taking out things to cook. I had no idea what to cook, so I just started putting shit together.

I decided to make him his favorite dish, steak with loaded mash potatoes, shrimp and broccoli on top, and a toss salad on the side. I also made sure to have his favorite drink ready, a cold Heineken.

As I cooked, I couldn't help but think about how much of a bitch ass nigga Marco was. He was out here doing me dirty with another bitch. But I'm here waiting on his ass to get home and he expects me to cook for him like nothing ever happened.

I felt like throwing the whole damn meal in the trash and telling him to go fuck himself. But something inside of me just couldn't let it go. Maybe it was the fact that I was pregnant with his baby, or maybe it was just my stupid ass thinking things would get better.

Whatever it was, I kept on cooking, making sure everything was perfect for when he got back. I had the table set, had his football game channel on and I just waited for him to get back. All of a sudden I heard the loud music, all I could say to myself is, "Marco home"

When Marco walked through the door, he smelled the food and his eyes lit up like a kid on Christmas morning,

"Damn Lyric, you cooked all of this?" he asked, sitting down at the table. "At least you good at something."

I just nodded, not saying a word. He started to eat, making sounds like he was in culinary heaven.

"Mmmmm this shit is good." he said, looking up at me with them sexy ass eyes.

But all I could see was the devil himself, sitting at the table, eating food I cooked for him. Marco finished eating, then he got up and walked into the living room, plopping himself down on the couch. He picked up the remote and started watching the game, acting like nothing was wrong.

"Lyric, get your ass over here," he yelled out, not even looking at me. "I need to talk to you about something."

I walked out of the kitchen into the living room, sitting down next to him on the couch. He turned to me, a smirk on his face.

"Look, I gotta leave tonight," he said, laughing in my face. "I gotta go visit my friend Tamara."

I raised an eyebrow, confused. "Who's that" I asked.

Marco chuckled, like he was enjoying some kinda private joke. "She's the mother of my daughter," he said.

My face fell to the floor, it felt like I'd been punched in the gut. "What?" I asked, trying to process what he just said.

He nodded, still smiling. "Yeah, my daughter was just born."

I felt like my heart was crushing inside my body. This nigga had another baby? And I'm sitting here pregnant with his child too.

"You got another baby?" I asked, trying to keep it cool.

Marco nodded again, like it was no big deal. "Yeah her name is Jasmine. She's a beauty."

I couldn't believe what I was hearing. This nigga had another whole family on the side. And I'm just sitting here, pregnant and clueless.

"How old is she?" I asked, trying to get more information.

Marco shrugged. "She's a few weeks old, Tamara just had her."

I felt like my world was crumbling down around me. This nigga had lied to me, cheated on me, and now he's telling me about another baby?

What about us?" I asked.

"There ain't no us," he said. "You just having my baby... that's it."Marco got up off the couch, laughing and just left.

The emotions sunk in... I'm nothing to this man. What did the lord have planned for me next? I just feel like giving up.

Chapter 11

Whew! Four months have passed and this baby got me big as a house. Feet swollen and the doctors say I'm high risk. It's summertime and I'm so hot, I can barely move without feeling like I'm gonna spontaneously combust.

I'm sitting here on the couch, watching some TV and eating ice-cream, trying to beat the heat. Marco is in the shower, getting himself cleaned up after working all morning... or whatever it is he does.

Haven't heard from any of my friends or my family in a while, so I decided to call my mom. We got a lot to catch up on, and I need some advice on how to deal with this pregnancy craziness.

"Hey Mom," I say, answering her concerned tone.

"Hey baby girl! How you doin'?" she asked.

"I'm good. Ma. Just. tired, and hot, and my back hurts like hell," I sighed, rubbing my belly.

"Lyric, you need to take care of yourself. You're high risk, and I don't want anything happening to you or the baby. You should be off your feet, not running around in this heat." she said, concerned.

"I am, Ma. I'm just sitting here chilling, Marco's in the shower. We're...we're doin' ok," I lied, not wanting to worry her more than she already was.

"Okay, baby. Just be careful, and don't let Marco stress you out. You hear me?" And don't let him put his hands on you... oh yeah news travels." she said.

I paused for a minute... "I am Ma. You don't have to worry about me." I said. "I'll talk to you later mom, love you."

"Love you too baby," she said back.

I hung up the phone and sat there for a moment, feeling a mix of emotions. I knew mom was worried, but I didn't know how to tell her everything that was going on. She would be on my ass and it would be a big mess over here. I just couldn't bring myself to do it.

Before I could dwell on it to long, Marco came out of the shower, looking fresh in his new outfit. "Yo, Lyric. I'm finna go out and do some shopping. Come on, let's go pick out some stuff for the baby," he said, smiling like he hadn't just put his hands on me a few days ago.

I looked at him, wishing I just had a gun and pop this nigga right in his head, but I know the lord wouldn't let me do that. I slowly got up from the couch, my back hurting bad, "Okay," I said, trying to sound casual.

We got in the car, and Marco started driving. He put his music on as usual, but his phone started ringing. He pulled his phone out his pocket and turned the music down low. He started talking, but I couldn't hear what he was saying. All I could hear was him saying, "Man, I'ma get you your money. " over and over again.

I didn't know what he was talking about, but I knew it couldn't be good. I just sat there, staring out the window, feeling like a big ass blow fish and Marco didn't pay me no mind. I didn't know what the future held, but I knew I had to protect myself and my baby.

As we drove, I couldn't help but think about how my life had turned out. I was pregnant and stuck in an abusive relationship, and isolated from everyone I loved. I knew I needed to make a change, but I just didn't know how.

And then, Marco's phone rang again. He answered it, and his whole demeanor changed. He started yelling, his voice raising with every word. "I told you, man, I'll handle it! You just worry bout your end, and I'll worry bout mine!"

I didn't know what was going on, but I knew that shit was probably about drugs. I just sat there silent, hoping that whatever it was wouldn't come back and haunt us.

After a while, Marco hung up the phone and looked at me. "Ain't nothin' to worry about, Lyric. Just some business bullshit," he said, trying to reassure me. This nigga just didn't know, I didn't give a fuck about what happen to him.

But I wasn't fooled. I knew Marco was in some kind of trouble, I knew it had to be something shady and I knew it was only a matter of time before it all came crashing down. All I could think about is my baby and our well being.

We pulled up at this clothing store called "Stacks & Stylez," and Marco got out, opening the door for me. I slowly got out and followed him inside. We walked through the aisles picking out clothes and toys for the baby. Marco acting like a different person, smiling and laughing like everything was all good.

But I kept my mind clear this time, I wasn't with his bullshit. I knew the real Marco, and I knew this was just a front. I played along though, not wanting to stir up nothing in public.

As we shopped, I couldn't help but think about the future. I knew I couldn't stay with Marco forever, but I just didn't know when I could escape. I was scared, and I just knew I was trapped. Things just had to change for the sake of the baby.

And as we left the store, I made a silent promise to myself: I was gonna get out, no matter what it took.

We walked to the car and Marco was moving really funny, looking all around and shit. We got in the car and Marco connected his phone to the radio, and the music was loud enough to drown my thoughts.

We were driving down the street, when Marco's phone began to ring again, breaking the silence. He glanced at the screen and hesitated for a second before answering.

"Yo," he said, his voice casual, like he was talking to one of his homies.

But then the voice on the other end changed everything. "Damn, don't you and your baby mama look good together," the guy said, his tone slick and menacing.

"You out shopping and shit, but you ain't got my fuckin' money."

Marco's expression shifted in an instant. He looked over me, his eyes narrowing, before focusing back on the road.

"Brah, hold on," he said, trying to be calm, but I could hear the tension in his voice. "Let me take this shit off bluetooth real quick."

But the man on the other end wasn't having it. "Nah, keep that shit on speaker," he said, his voice all deep and shit. "You got 24 hours to get my money, or Ima have fun killing you, you girl, and your baby."

My heart damn near dropped. I couldn't say anything, I was just frozen with fear. Marco turned red with rage, but he wasn't saying anything back.He just hung up the phone and slammed his fist on the steering wheel.

"Fuck!" he yelled, his anger echoing through the car.

I still couldn't speak. My mind was going 100 miles per hour. Who was this due? What did Marco get himself into now? And why was he involving me and the baby in this shit?

We pulled up to the house, and I got out of the car still trying to process that shit that just went down. I got to the door and unlocked it and stepped foot in the apartment. Marco came in dead behind me all paranoid and shit.

"Look, I fucked up," he said, his voice low and urgent. "And you're gonna have to help me get this money up ASAP."

I looked at him with a stank face, my eyes rolling and everything. "Marco, what the fuck am I suppose to do? I asked him, my voice dripping with attitude. "And I'm 4 months pregnant, ain't no way I can be doing anything out there."

Marco's expression changed in an instant. He got upset, his face twisted in anger. And before I could even react, he slapped me.

"Bitch, we ain't got time for this shit." he yelled at me. "You're gonna go in the back and get yourself fresh while I get the stuff out the car. Have your ass in something real sexy."

I was stunned, my check stinging from the slap. But I knew better than to mess with Marco when he was like this. So I turned around and headed to the back room, tears streaming down my face.

As I got ready, my mind was racing. What was Marco planning? What did he need me to do? And how was I gonna get us outta this mess?

I put on a nice sexy dress and my sexy Gucci sandals, just like Marco told me to. And when I came out into the living room, he looked me up and down like a piece of meat.

I sat on the couch, looking all sexy even though I was pregnant. Marco was gazing at me, a sly grin spreading across his face. "You understood the assignment," he said, his voice low and husky.

I nodded, trying to just go along with him and I was feeling more and more uncomfortable by the minute. Just as I thought things couldn't get any worse, a knock came at the door. Marco got up to answer it, and I heard him dapping some dude up.

"Who the fuck is this?" I thought to myself as Marco walked back into the living room with this random nigga . Marco walked over to me and said, "Lyric, this my homie Tre from around the way. Tre, this Lyric."

I just nodded, trying not to show any emotions. Tre looked like a straight-up thug, all tatted up and whatnot. Marco asked him if he had the money, and Tre said yeah.

"I'm so lost," I thought to myself. What the fuck was going on? Why did Marco invite this dude over if he wanted me to get all sexy for him?

Then Marco dropped the bombshell. "Lyric, take my homie Tre in the room and pay him for the money," he said.

I couldn't believe this muthafucka. He wanted me to fuck this nigga for some money. I was shocked, but I knew better than to say anything. If I didn't, Marco would knock me upside my damn head.

I walked toward the room and Tre followed behind me. I can tell that he was all into this shit, because he was saying "Mmmm" as he followed me. I stepped into the room, it smelled like stale weed and desperation. I walked toward the door and tried to close it.

"Leave the fuckin' door open," Marco said all rude and shit.

I glanced at Marco and he had this devilish look in his eyes. I didn't want to do this shit, but I wasn't trying to die either. Tre started to slide his hands up my thighs, my stomach twisted, but Marco's eyes - cold as a winter curb, locked with me from the doorway.

"Ain't got all day, Lyric," he growled, flocking his chin at Tre. "Get to it."

Tre grinned, gold tooth glinting like a warning. "Y'all pregnant bitches always tight as hell," he mumbled, yanking my dress up rough. I sucked in a breath, my nails clawing the mattress. *Fuck this. Fuck him. Fuck Marco.*

"Hurry yo' ass up," Marco barked, firing up a blunt like this was a Netflix show.

Tre didn't waste time. He bent me over on the bed, I almost fell on my stomach. He pulled out his dick and put it inside of me.

Every thrust felt like a punch, his grunts loud in my ear. "Damn, Marco," he huffed, sweating all over my back. "Yo bitch worth every dime."

Marco laughed like this shit was funny.

"Told you she'd handle business," he said, blowing smoke at the ceiling.

I squeezed my eyes shut, my mind screaming at me to run. But where? Marco always finds me, he always finds me. And when he finds me he makes my face look like I've been fighting in a boxing ring.

Tre finished quick, zipping his pants up like nothing happened. Tre tossed Marco another stack of cash, and told him he would call him later. Marco then looked at me in disgust with his nose turned up.

"Clean yo' self up," he yelled. "We got somewhere to go.

I walked into the bathroom to clean myself up, I scrubbed between my legs, the water turning cloudy as Tre's stank rinsed down the drain. My reflection in the mirror looked broken - swollen eyes, bruised and black. I missed my old life and the person standing here was not me.

Marco banged on the door. "Lyric! We gotta move! Slim ain't playin'!"

I pulled my panties up, my thighs still shaking, and I pulled my dress down and opened the door. Marco stood there, duffle bag slung over his shoulder, cash barely zipped inside.

"The fuck you standing there like That for?"he snapped. "Ain't like you ain't done this before. Now come on." He yelled.

We left the apartment and got into the car. The car reeked of a bitches cheap ass perfume, but I wasn't gonna say anything. My stomach churned, my hands clamped over my bump like I could shield the baby from the bullshit ahead. Marco's knuckles whiten on the wheel, and I just kept looking at him, lord I was scared as fuck and just wanted out of this.

Not knowing where the hell we are going, I just started praying. Praying that God keeps me and my baby safe, because lord knows Marco didn't give fuck.

Chapter 12

Marco's whip crawled through Renderson County like a roach on probation, his fingers trembling on the wheel, I can tell he was nervous as fuck. Five blocks to Slim's spot. Five blocks between me and a body bag. My palms sweat into the leather seats, my baby bump pressing against the seatbelt...my fat ass couldn't breath.

"Bitch, you hear me?" Marko barked, flicking ashes out the window. "Walk in there mute. Look at the floor. Breathe too loud, and I will punch you dead in yo' airway."

I didn't flinch. I just stared at the Glock that was under his seat. Four months pregnant, 17 rounds, One chance. I got to leave this nigga asap, this is not love at all.

We turned in on Bodersville road and the neighborhood looked terrible. The streets looked like a zombie hood flick - bodega gates rusted shut, crackheads huddled over fires in trash cans, stray cats hissing at shadows. Marco cut on the lights, coasting past Slim's goons leaning on a red Camry. "The fuck they do out here?" I mumbled.

"Shut Up." Marco's jaw clenched. "Ain't yo' business."

A dude in a ski mask tapped our hood with a bat. "Aye, Marco! Slim said hurry yo' ass up!"

The block got quiet. Too quiet. Porch lights flickered off as we rolled by. My phone buzzed - a text from Passion: "WHERE U AT???" I thumb-deleted it. No loose ends.

Marco's knee bounced like a jackhammer. "Slim, ask about the money, let me talk. You just stand there and look stupid like always."

"Ain't gotta act," I shot back.

He side-eyed me, grip tightening on the wheel. "Try me, Lyric. I'll dump yo' body in the East River. Pregnant bitches sink faster." he laughed.

Slim's trap house sagged like a drunk, piss-yellow paint peeling on the boards. A pit bull named Bolo choked his chain, foaming at us.

"The fuck he feed that thing?" I muttered.

"Bodies," Marco said, killing the engine. "Move."

I got out of the car and shut the door, waiting for Marco to lead the way. Slim's goons parted like the Red Sea, grinning at my stomach.

"Aye, Marco! You pimpin' pregnant bitches now?"

Marco just looked at them and kept on walking. We got to the door and Marco knocked, Slim answered the door shirtless, tatts everywhere on his chest.

"You late nigga," he spat, the smell of henny on his breath and it stanked. "And why the fuck you bringing pregnant bitches to my spot? Brah, get ya ass in here, you trippin'?"

We entered his home and I felt like I was in a warzone-cash stacks, crack pipes, and a half-eaten bucket of KFC sat on the table. Slim's boy, Snake snatched the bag from Marco and ripped it open and started counting it.

" Hold on brah," Snake said. "You 5k short, boss."

Slime's smile died. "You tryna get buried, Marco?"

Marco stepped back, rubbing his hands together. "I got the rest tonight! Swear on my–"

"ON YOUR MAMA?" Slim lunged, slamming Marco into the wall. "Yo' mama dead cause you ain't pay me last time!"

My stomach dropped. Marco got his own mama smoked? What the fuck this nigga got going on? This shit ain't the first time, and he still dealing with people who killed his mom's?"

First time I had seen Marco quiet as fuck...shit I was even scared. I don't know what is going to happen tonight. Before I could even process that thought.

Slim walked over toward me, Marco eyes dead on him. Slim pressed his burner to my belly. "See this is how everythang gonna play out. New deal. She stays here. You bring my cash by midnight..." He cocked his gun back. "Or I'ma paint these ways with yo' baby's brains."

Marco Froze, sweat dripping off his nose. "Slim, c'mom–" he begged.

"OR I POP YO ASS NOW!" Slim screamed, standing up spitting in Marco's face. "Your choice nigga!"

Marco's eyes met mine cold, empty, dead."...I'll be back."

He bolted. The door slammed. Slim laughed, dragging me to a crusty ass couch. "He ain't coming back," he whispered.

Slim's eye's narrowed on my busted lip, and my black eye that was bruised by Marco earlier. "The fuck happened to yo' face?" he asked, voice cutting through the silence like a shank.

I swallowed hard, my throat tight. *Think. Lie. Survive.* "Fell," I mumbled, eyes glued to the floor.

"Fell?" Slim leaned back, laughing sharp as gunfire. "Bitch, you fell" on what? That niggas fist? You wanna be with a nigga who treats you like a this?"

My chest heaved. *This a test? A trap?* "I...I don't–"

"You don't *what?*" Slim leaned in, gold tooth catching the light. "Let me school you – Marco's been snitching to feds. Rat-ass-nigga. Lost respect for him *long* time ago."

My head snapped up. *Snitch?* Marco's been calling me disloyal for months. "He...he what?"

Slim smirked. "Yeah. So here's the play–you help me bury this nigga, I helped you get your life back? Want out?"

"My mouth went dry. *Trust slim?* But the bruises on my ribs screamed *yes.* "I...I don't wanna be with him," I whispered, tears started to run down my face. "He beats me for nothing. Took...took everything from me."

Slim nodded to his boy, who ducked into the backroom. The dude came back with a big red bag and handed it to Slim. Slim then opens it up and looks at me.

"Aight." He said pulling out a burner phone and a stack of twenties from a Nike box, sliding them across the table. "Take this. Number's already saved. Call when he's sleepin', at work, whenever. I'll handle the rest."

I stuffed the phone and cash into my jacket, hands shaking. "Why you helping me?"

"Cause I don't fuck with snitches," he said, shrugging. "And a fine ass pregnant female like yo'self deserves better than Marco's dusty ass. He can't even handle the street life, what he does is a front."

I couldn't say anything, I was speechless. Then there was a knock on the door, and the door crashed open. Marco stormed in, sweating bullets, another duffle bag slung over his shoulder.

"Got yo' money," he said, tossing it at Slim's feet. "Now let's go, Lyric."

Slim's boy counted the cash slow, like he was savoring Marco's panic.

"All here, boss." Snake said.

Slim stood, towering over Marco. "You lucky I'm feelin' generous." he jerked his chin at me." "Take yo' bitch and bounce. But play me again?" he tapped his glock. "I'ma airmail yo' soul."

Marco grabbed my arm, yanking me toward the door. "Move, Lyric." Marco said. I glanced back at Slim, he nodded, almost imperceptible. *Soon*.

The ride back to the apartment felt like a death march. Marco sped through red lights, his fingers strangling the steering wheel like it owed him money.

"The fuck Slim was whispering to you?" he yelled, cutting his eyes at me.

I kept my head down, clutching my belly like it could armor me from the rage.

"You told me to keep my mouth shut…" I muttered. "Had a gun to my head the whole time."

"And?" He smacked the wheel. "You look like you wanted to stay! What, you fuck' dat slow ass nigga too?!"

"N-no–"

"STUTTER AGAIN, I'll BREAK YO' JAW!" He swerved into the apartment lot, tires screaming. "Get the fuck out." he yelled.

I got out the car and shuffled inside, my back throbbing like I'd been hit by a bus. The baby kicked hard, like it knew the world it was coming into was trash. All I wanted was my bed, a jar of pickles, and that pint of mint chip ice cream I'd hidden in the freezer. But Marco stormed past me, flopping on the couch and pulling out a fat wad of cash.

"That nigga Slim dumb as fuck," he laughed to himself, thumbing through the bills. "Thought he got one over on me? I swapped his money out with that counterfeit shit.

My stomach dropped. *Counterfeit?* Slim would skin his ass for that.

Marco's phone buzzed. He answered, slick-grinning. "Yo...Yeah dat nigga took the bait. We good." He paused, eyes sliding to me. "Nah, she ain't a problem. That bitch ain't that stupid."

I froze. *Who's he talkin' to? Cops? Rivals?*

"The fuck you staring at?" Marco snapped, covering the receiver. "Take ya ass in the room!"

I limped to the bedroom, my mind racing. The burner phone felt like a brick in my jacket. I needed to stash it *now*.

Kneeling slow, I pried up the loose floorboard under the bed - my secret vault for runaway cash, a switchblade, and pregnancy test I'd kept like a fucked-up souvenir. I slid the burner phone and Slim's cash inside, replacing the board and kicking my sneakers over it.

The door flew open. The fuck you doing?" Marco stood there, eyes wild.

"My back hurt," I lied, wincing as I stood. "Just taking my shoes off."

He stepped closer, reeking of Vodka and hate. "You ain't slick, Lyric. I see you squirming"

"I'm pregnant Marco!" I said.

"AND?" He grabbed my arm, yanking me up. "You my bitch first." His free hand slid down my hip. "I need some stress relief. Get naked."

I froze. "Marco, the baby and I are tired—"

"THE BABY AIN'T HERE YET!" He shoved me onto the bed, unbuckling his belt. "You think I give a fuck about how you feel?"

Tears blurred my vision as he forced himself on me, he didn't care if he had hurt the baby or not. I turned over and my eyes locked to the floorboard. *The burner. Slim. Revenge.*

Marco finished quick, zipping up his jeans like nothing happened. "Don't move," he ordered, flopping next to me. "I'm sleeping' here tonight."

I laid right there beside him, staring at the floorboard praying that the phone didn't go off. I just laid there hurting badly and fell asleep.

The next morning, sunlight stabbed through the blinds, the morning birds were

chirping, and the energy felt like love. Marco
was still knocked out the bed, snoring like a
chainsaw, one arm slung over his face. I slid
out slowly, my bare feet hitting the cold floor.
Burner first. Pee second.

I crouched by the loose floorboard,
prying it up quietly as a church mouse. The
burner phone blinked with a text:

Slim: U alive? Plan's on. If he touch you,
we body dat nigga before breakfast.

I breathed for the first time all morning.
Safe. For now.

I tiptoed to the bathroom, locking the
door and cranking the sink faucet to drown out
the noise. Sat on the toilet, pissing, felt like my
bladder was about to burst.

Me: Alive. Appointment @ 11. I'll text
you later."

Slim: Bet. If that nigga hurt you. It will
gonna be worse for that nigga."

I flushed the toilet, washed my hands,
and splashed water on my face. The mirror
showed ghost-dark circles, chapped lips, baby
bump looking like a basketball under my
clothes. *Keep it together.*

I walked out the bathroom and glanced
at Marco, he was still knocked out. I went into
the kitchen and started to prepare breakfast. I
had the kitchen starting to smell like hope for

two seconds, thick-cut bacon sizzling, scrambled eggs with cheese fluffy as clouds, toast buttered golden. I even cracked open a can of cinnamon rolls, Marco's favorite, just to keep his dumb ass calm. The radio played some old Mary J. Blige, it was like God was trying to give me strength.

Knife in drawer. Syrup on the counter. Gun in Marco's waistband. I memorized it all.

"LYRIC!" His voice boomed down the hall. "WHERE THE FUCK YOU AT?!"

"Kitchen!" I shouted back, plastering on a smile.

He stomped in, shirtless, jeans sagging, eyes bloodshot red. "Smells descent," he grunted, snatching a strip of bacon off the plate.

"I'm hitting the block today. Meeting Tre and the boys about this job."

I froze, spatula mid-air. "But...my doctor's appointment at 11. For the baby."

He smirked, biting into the bacon. "Ain't my problem. Baby ain't here yet."

"They gotta check the gender and the heartbeat–"

"GENDER?" He slammed his fist on the counter, syrup bottles falling. "The fuck you wanna know the gender for? You tryna jinx my baby or something?"

I bit my tongue." *It's a girl. I know it."* I said.

"After that appointment," he said, snatching the spatula, "come scoop me from Tre's spot. I'ma send you the location. Don't keep me waiting."

"What if the doctor's late?"

He leaned in, bacon breathe hot on my face. "Then *run*. Or I'ma give you something to really cry about."

Marco headed to the bathroom to take a shower, I slid the burner outta my bra:

Me: Heading to my appointment. A lot you don't know, tell you about it later.

Slim: He hurt you? I'll kill him first.

I tucked the phone back, my hands steady shaking, and headed out to my appointment. Lord let everything be alright with my baby.

Chapter 13

The car stereo blasted my high vibration music–as I cruised down Flatbush Ave, smiling so hard my cheeks hurt. Sunlight poured through the windshield, very warm on my skin, and for the first time in months, I felt...*light*. Like maybe me and my baby could fly right out this nightmare.

Then Marco's name lit up my phone screen.

"Damn, you ain't made it to your destination yet?" he yelled, no "hello," no nothing.

I squeezed the wheel hard. *This nigga think I'm driving a goddamn jet?*

"No, Marco, I'm not there yet...almost."

"Don't try no fuck shit," he snapped. "Yo' location on. I see everything."

"Okay, Marco." *Click.*

"AAAAARGH!" I screamed, slapping the dashboard. *How this man turn sunshine into sewage in two seconds?*

I pulled into the parking lot of the clinic and calmed myself down. I got out the car slowly and walked into the building, my lower back was killing me. The receptionist smiled too sweet, like she knew my life was trash. "Good Morning my name is..." but before I could say it she started talking.

"Lyric, right? Have a seat. Dr. Taylor will be right with you."

The waiting room was full of happy couples - niggas rubbing bellies, girls laughing over ultrasound pics. *"Why can't that be me?"* I sank into a chair, clutching my jacket around my bump like armor.

Before I could get comfortable, the nurse called me back, took my blood pressure, and side-eyed the bruise on my wrist.

"You safe at home, honey?"

"I'm good," I lied, voice flat. *Save it, Karen.*

In the exam room, Marco's face popped up on my screen again. I had to answer right away.

"WHERE THE FUCK YOU AT? WHY YOU WHISPERING'?"

"I'm at the doctor's, Marco. Check the location," I hissed, and he hung up before he could curse me out.

I sat in the exam room waiting on the doctor to come in. All I wanted to do was just pack my clothes and just leave. This man was my worst nightmare that ruined my whole life.

But before I could get deep into my thoughts, Dr. Taylor knocked on the door and floated in like an angel in a lab coat.

"Hello, Lyric," she said with a smile. "How are we feeling?"

"Hurting... A lot." I responded.

She frowned, gliding the ultrasound machine to the side of the curtain and picking up the wand and placing the gel on it.

"This is going to be a little cold, Ok." she said.

I just nodded my head because I was nervous about everything. She glanced at me and she was just a happy lady.

"First pregnancy?" she said.

"Yeah." I mumbled.

"Well, you're measuring 27 weeks now." she said with a smile.

I sat up so fast, the paper on the bed had crinkled up. "But...I thought I was 4 months!"

"Oh no Lyric, You're six months."

Six months. Marco's fists. Marco's lies. "*You ain't shit without me.*" Through all this stuff with this man and all the times he had beat me, I was pregnant the whole time.

"Lyric would you like to know the sex of your baby?" Dr. Taylor stated.

"YES." I said with excitement.

Dr. Taylor pointed at the screen. "See that? That shape right there. That's your babygirl."

Tears flooded my eyes. *A daughter.* A tiny soul I'd die to protect. I have a mini me growing inside of me and she is hearing everything her mommy is going through. I can't let my baby be raised like this.

"Ok, lyric you are good to go. I sent you some prenatal vitamins to the pharmacy. Make sure you are taking them everyday as I prescribed, and I want to see you back here in 3 weeks, ok?"

"Ok," I responded back. "See you later."

I walked to the front desk to grab my follow up appointment card and headed to the car. I got in the car and sat in the parking lot for a minute, ultrasound clutched to my chest, and I dialed Marco up.

"Bout time," he answered. "Scoop me from Tre spot now. "

"Marco...it's a girl."

Silence. Then: *fuck* I care? Get here fast or it's not gonna be a good day for yo' ass."
Click.

I stared at the ultrasound for a minute. "He ain't gonna hurt you." I whispered. "I promise."

I started the car and headed out to get Marco. The steering wheel burned under my grip as I headed up toward Tre's block, feeling real good blasting "Savage" in the speakers like a battle anthem. My baby girl started kicking like she knew Mama was happy. "We almost free, baby," I whispered, rubbing my belly. "Ain't gonna let that nigga hurt us no more."

As I pulled up to Tre's house, Marco stood outside leaning on a busted Honda with his boys, smirking like he'd just won the fucking lottery. His eyes cut to me as I pulled up, and he dapped Tre up and then he got into the car.

"Bout time, slow-ass bitch," he yelled, yanking the car door open. "You drive like my grandma." I just kept my mouth close and I started driving home.

I bit my tongue so hard I tasted pennies. *Six months pregnant. Six months of this nigga's bullshit."*

"Stop at the ABC store," he ordered, pointing at the store like I was his Uber driver. "And hurry up. I ain't got all day."

I parked, watching him walk into the store. The clerk flinched when he saw Marco slam his money stack on the counter. This nigga spending Slim's money– and bought a big bottle of Remy. Cracked it open before hitting the door, took a swig, then stumbled back to the car, liquor dripping down his shirt.

"Drive," he slurred, spilling cognac on the seats. "And fix yo' face. Look like you smelling piss."

I just kept on driving , just ignoring his ignorant ass. We pulled up to the apartment, and there was a female–perched on the curb like a vulture in booty shorts. Baby hairs crispy, lashes thick as jail bars and just ugly as fuck.

"Who the fuck is that?" I said, parking so hard the tires screamed.

Marco smirked, adjusting his jeans like he was packing a cannon.

"Relax. She's just here to kick it."

"In my house? I said. "Marco, I'm so tired of the disrespect."

"You mean my house." he corrected, snatching the keys. "You sleeping on the couch tonight. Me and shawty need privacy."

Marco got out of the car with my keys and he slammed the door. The girl strutted over, smiling like she'd won the Powerball.

"Hey, daddy!"

"What's good, ma?" Marco said as he wrapped his arm around her waist, whispering some nasty shit in her ear. She giggled, eyeing my belly as I got out of the car.

"Damn, girl," she said, smacking her gum. "You let him rawdog you?"

I rolled my fucking eyes and ignored that bitch, not even giving her the satisfaction of a response. Marco walked in front of me, with his arm still wrapped around her waist, and I could feel anger shimmering just below my surface. As we entered my apartment, she started twerking and shaking her ass, and Marco smacking her ass, making her squeal with delight. I was disgusted by their blatant disrespect.

"What the fuck is wrong with you, Marco?" I thought to myself. "You bring this hoe into our home and think you can just get away with it."

I kicked off my shoes as soon as I stepped in the living room, relieved to be free from the tight confines of my swollen feet. Marco looked at me laughing , like the shit he was doing was ok.

"We're gonna go in the bedroom, You pregnant ass know where everythang at. Shit, this is yo' place. right?"

Him and his little side piece hoe started laughing in my face and joking around, like they were the ones who lived here.

As soon as they closed the door behind them, I sat down on the couch and grabbed the burner phone from my jacket. I quickly texted Slim, filling him in on what had been going on with Marco.

"Hey Slim, it's me. I got some news for you. Marco gave you counterfeit money and now he's spending your real money like it's going outta style. That nigga had the nerve to bring a bitch to my house, he is a fucking snake ass nigga."

Just as I hit send on the text message, I heard Marco and that bitch having sex in my muthafuckin' room. The sound of their moans and laughter made my blood boil, the baby even started kicking.

"This muthafucka got some nerves," I thought to myself. "He's fuckin' some random bitch in my bed while I'm sitting here pregnant with his child? That shit ain't right."

The disrespect was real. He had no respect for me or our unborn baby. All he cared about was getting his dick wet with whoever would have him. The more I listened to them fucking like a couple of wild animals in heat, the more furious I became.

"Marco is the real bitch in this relationship," I said out loud to myself.

My mind started racing, thinking about all sorts of ways to get back at him for this betrayal. How could he do this to me? Did he really think he could bring some random hoe into our home and disrespect me like this? The fire burning inside me only grew stronger with each passing moment.

And then it hit me - an idea so diabolical that even I had to admit it was genius. A plan began forming in my mind to take care of both Marco's side piece and his fake ass all at once... that shit was gonna be epic.

"Marco thinks he can play with me and his unborn child?" I thought to myself, a sly smile spreading across my face. "He thinks he can cheat on me and get away with it? Nah, that nigga got another thing coming."

I got up off the sofa, grabbing my shoes and heading out to the car. I was over hearing this shit for right now. I got into the car and I pulled out of the parking lot and hit the streets. My mind raced with thoughts of how I was gonna get back at him.

As I drove down the street, I grabbed my burner phone and dialed Slim's number. He answered on the first ring, no hesitation.

"Yo, wassup queen?" He said.

I didn't waste no time, got straight to the point.

"I really need to talk to you ASAP, Slim. Marco made me turn my location on, so he can see every move I make." I stated.

Slim's tone turned serious.

"Aight bet. Meet me at the grocery store on the corner of Hilton Avenue. You can play it off like you needed to get something you forgot." He said.

I agreed and then I hung up the phone. I pulled up into the parking lot of the store, I took my time getting out of the car. Still hurting like hell, I walked into the store and grabbed a cart, heading straight for the pickles section. As I walked down the aisle, Slim came up behind me.

"What's good Lyric?" he whispered in my ear. We started talking, keeping our voices low so nobody would overhear us discussing Marco's sorry ass.

"Yea, dat nigga think he can play me," Slim said shaking his head. "We scanned that counterfeit cash he gave me and seen that nigga tried to play me dirty. Now this shit has gotten serious."

I nodded in agreement, filling him in on all the details of what happened when Marco brought me home that night. Slim listened intently, his face getting tighter by the minute.

"Aight Lyric, finish shopping, head home and just wait for my text," he instructed me before turning around and walking out the store, disappearing in the air like a ghost.

I finished shopping, grabbing some ice cream sandwiches since they were on sale for a 2 for $5 deal, then I headed home with music blasting through the speakers. Hit Em Up playing and I'm thinking about how that abusive muthafucka at that house is going to pay me for everything he has done to me.

I pulled back up to the apartment, parking the car and sitting there for a minute, collecting my thoughts. I was an emotional mess, still trying to process how the man I loved could be putting me through so much hurt. I took a deep breath, grabbed my bags and got out of the car.

As I walked into the apartment, I was trying to keep it together, but it was hard. I started putting away my things, trying to distract myself from the pain and anger that was building up inside me.

Just as I was putting the ice cream sandwiches in the freezer, Marco popped out of the room, faced all balled up and mean mugging me.

"Where the fuck you been?" he asked, his tone all rude and shit. "And you better have a good fucking reason for living like that."

Chapter 14

I tried to explain, my voice shaking slightly. "Marco, I swear, I just had to run to the store and get something I was craving. The baby kickin' me so hard it started to hurt. I just needed to get outta here for a minute and clear my head."

But Marco wasn't having it. His eyes narrowed, his face twisted in anger, just mean mugging me and shit.

"Lyric, I swear to God, you better not let me find out some other shit," he growled, his hand reaching out and grabbing my neck.

I felt a surge of fear as he started choking me, his grip tight and unyielding. "Marco, you're hurting me," I gasped, trying to pry his fingers loose.

But Marco just laughed, his eyes gleaming with a crazy intensity. "Bitch, I don't give a fuck about hurting you," he yelled. "You better be lucky you're still breathing in this bitch."

He let my neck go abruptly, and I stumbled back, gasping for air. My heart was racing, my mind reeling from the shock of what just happened. But as I looked into Marco's eyes, I saw something there that chilled me to the bone - a cold, calculating hatred that made me realize I was in grave danger.

I stood there, still trying to process the hurtful shit that had just come out of Marco's mouth. "Now get in here and fix me somethin' to eat, that baby can fuckin' wait, shit … that baby probably not even mine anyway." he said, laughing like that shit was hilarious.

I felt like going out again, finding a gun and coming back here and shooting both of these muthafuckas, but I knew I had to keep it together. I took a deep breath and tried to shake off the hurt, focusing on cooking dinner instead. I headed into the kitchen, my mind on 1000 with thoughts of getting out of this bullshit.

As I started cooking, the aroma of fried chicken, turnips, macaroni and cheese, and biscuits filled the apartment. My stomach growled at the delicious smell, but my heart was still heavy.

Marco eventually emerged from the room with that bitch on his arms. He walked into the kitchen, sniffing the air like a dog.

"Mmm, something smells good in here," he said, his eyes lighting up with anticipation.

I kept my back turned to him, trying not to show him how much his words had hurt me. "It's just dinner, asshole," I said flatly.

Marco walked over to me, his eyes roaming over my body like he ain't never met me before. "You know what would go good with this?" he asked, grinning like the sneaky nigga he was.

I shook my head no, but inside I was thinking what the fuck now.

"Some fucking good ass beer." He said as he sat down at the table and started eating without even saying thank you or anything. He just dug in like a savage animal devouring every last bite on his plate then got up and got another plate then did the same thing again.

After finishing both plates he let out a big belch showing no respect for nobody. Then he turned around and told that bitch to come eat with him, and she came running in. She sat down where I was supposed to sit and he laughed and told her to help herself. She did exactly what this nigga told her to do, they jus sat there laughing and talking like they were the only two people in this damn house.

Meanwhile I'm standing there feeling like a fool watching them eat my cooking without even being invited to sit down or anything. I started to walk over and grab me a plate and fix it, but then Marco looked at me with a grin.

"Hell nah, you don't need to sit over wit us, you can just start cleaning up this mess." He said, adding on to the hurt I'm already going through. "By the way, bitch you aint shit without me."

I was stuck in the kitchen, cleaning up the mess from dinner, my stomach growling with hunger. This nigga really wanted to jeopardize me and his daughter's life for this bitch. I was fed up with this shit.

Before I knew it, the burner phone started ringing. Damn, I forgot to turn it back on silence. Marco glanced over at me, and all I could is just stand there, knowing I done fucked up.

"What the fuck was that?" Marco said.

I tried to play it off with him, "Oh my phone was ringing, probably Passion or my mom calling me."

Marco glanced over at the living room table and saw my phone. "How the fuck is that possible, and your phone is right there on the fucking table? Now, Lyric, what the fuck was that?" I couldn't say nothing, I was stuck, I was caught and didn't know what was going to happen.

Marco came rushing toward me and pulled my clothes, and that's when the burner phone fell out of my shirt. He looked down at the floor and then looked at me and smacked me.

"Bitch, what the fuck is this?" he said while trying to look into it, but it was locked.

Marco, please, I'm pregnant," I said to him. "I'm begging you, please."

He grabbed me by the collar of my shirt and said, "Bitch, you been playing me this whole muthafuckin' time. Get ya ass in the bedroom now."

I walked into the room, and all I could do was pray. He told the other girl that she needed to stay out there and stay put but turn the Tv volume up. The girl looked up at him and said, "yes daddy."

That's when Marco stormed into the room and made eye contact with me. All he could say is "Bitch, I warned you to not fuck with me." And that's when it all happened.

He started beating me like a rag doll. Punches were flying, kicks were landing, and slaps were cracking. My body went numb as he continued to assault on my fragile body.

"Bitch! You think you can play games with Me!" Marco roared as his fists rained down on me more.

My cries of pain filled the air but only seemed to fuel Marco further!

After a few minutes which felt like hours, Marco stopped, finally exhausted himself , as I laid there broken, battered, unable to move or speak. I just knew he was going to leave me there to die.

Marco walked back into the living room, closing the door behind him. He started talking to the other bitch and firing up a blunt. Just as he was lightening it, a car pulled up. He didn't know who it was, so he just sat there with that bitch in his arms until there was a knock on the door.

"Who is it?" Marco said.

"It's me, nigga. Open the fucking door," Slim responded.

Marco walked to the door and opened it like nothing had gone down.

"Wassup up, my nigga?" he said, letting Slim and his two homies in.

"I just stopped by to see how business is going for you nigga," Slim said.

Marco smiled, trying to play it cool. "Shit, everythang going aight. Just trying to chill with my new ol' lady and shit before we go out to eat."

Slim looked at Marco with a mixture of disgust and anger, his eyes scanning the room for any sign of me. "Damn brah, what the fuck happened to yo' hands?" Slim asked, looking at Marco's bruised and bloody knuckles.

Marco hurried up and made up a lie. "Shit, this nigga owed me some money and shit, and I had to rough him up... you know how it is." Slim already knew this nigga was lying and was already upset about his money. His face turned red with rage as he took a step closer to Marco.

"You think you can play me like that?" Slim said, his voice low and menacing. "You think you can give me fake counterfeit shit and get away with it?"

Slim pulled out his glock and pointed it at Marco. "Nigga, you tried to give me counterfeit shit trying to get me caught. Now ya ass about to pay for dat shit." Slim and his homies started beating the fuck out of Marco with their fists and pistols. They beat him until he was bloody and bruised.

Finally slim let him up. "Where the fuck is Lyric at?" he asked again.

This time, Marco still didn't say shit. Slim gave his niggas the head nod to finish beating Marco's ass while he glanced over at the bitch on the couch, and put the gun to her head.

"Bitch do you wanna die today?" Slim said.

The girl looked at him shaking and scared and stuttered no. "Then where the fuck is Lyric at? Slim demanded. Scared as hell, the girl pointed to the room where I was lying badly beaten...

Slim walked into the room where I laid motionless on the floor, his eyes widened in shock, he rushed over to me.

"No No No, Lyric get up!" he yelled. "Yo, lyric get the fuck up ma. Yo' y'all come help me get her outta here."

His homies rushed in there to my badly beaten body and that's when they picked me up and put me in the car and rushed me to the hospital. They got me in the car and they drove as fast as they could.

"Stay with me Lyric, you got to be strong for you and that baby." Slim said to me.

They took me to the nearest hospital down the street. As Slim and his boys rushed me into the hospital. Slim yelled out to me:

"Lyric, stay with me, queen! Keep your eyes open!" he said, as the sound of sirens filled the air as we sped through the streets.

We finally arrived at the hospital, and Slim's homies jumped out the car, screaming for help.

"We need some fucking help in here!" they yelled at the nurses.

The medical staff quickly sprang into action, surrounding me with a flurry of activity. They started hooking me up to machines and injecting me with medication.

Slim was by my side, holding my hand and talking to me.

"Lyric, baby, please don't leave me. I'm so sorry I didn't get here sooner."

The doctors and nurses worked on me for what felt like hours, but I was still unresponsive. My baby and I were in stable condition, but it was clear that we had been through a traumatic experience.

Meanwhile, Slim and his boys were furious. They left the hospital, determined to find Marco and make him pay for what he had done. They got back in their cars and sped off, not giving a fuck about the police.

As they arrived back at the apartment complex where Marco had left me to die, they were already prepared. They had their guns drawn looking everywhere but there was no sign of Marco anywhere, Slim went ape yelling at the top of his lungs.

"FUUUCCCKKK!"

Slim and his boys just didn't know Marco was outside of the apartment, watching them outside in the car. He saw them searching everyone room and watching every move they made.

"Them muthafuckas stupid," he said to himself, with a sly grin spreading across his face as he sat in the car grunting in pain with his new bitch.

He was trying to be smart, knowing that Slim and his boys would be looking for him. They knew what car I drove and what car Marco drove, so he switched it up thinking he could outsmart them and drive his new bitch car.

The girl looked at him with concern, seeing the bruises and blood on his face. "What do we do now, daddy?" she asked.

Marco looked at her, still hurting from the beating he took. "Just ride with me, ma," he said, starting the car and driving off into the night. All she did was look at him smiling.

"Ok, daddy"

She didn't know what kind of plans Marco had up his sleeves, but she didn't care... she was just another stupid girl that Marco had rigged in like a fish with his lame as pick up lines... yeap...the same lines that he used on me and the club.

Back at the hospital, I lay unconscious, fighting hard not to die, me and my baby girl.

Somehow the news traveled and my mom received a call saying that I was rushed to the hospital. She didn't waste no time, she jumped in her car and rushed over to the hospital.

Meanwhile, Marco had other plans. He snuck into the hospital, dressed up and fake crying. He walked around and walked around until he finally stopped by the front desk to speak with the nurse there.

"Excuse me," he said. "I'm looking for my sister, Lyric Williams. She was brought in here earlier." he explained.

The nurse looked up at her phone, slightly annoyed at the interruption. "Okay...let me check," she said slowly, typing away on her computer.

Marco tried to appear anxious, tapping his foot impatiently on the floor. "Can you please hurry? I'm worried about her." He stated.

The nurse finally figured everything out. "Ok sir, your sister is in room 119, but please be cautious she is in stable condition." She responded. Marco smiled and headed straight to my room.

About 10 minutes later, My mom and brother arrived at the same time, searching high and low frantically. They rushed to the front desk where the nurse was, they were worried sick about me.

"Excuse me," my mom said, "I'm trying to get someone's attention. "We're looking for my daughter, Lyric Williams. She was brought here earlier.

The nurse sighed, rolling her eyes. "I'm checking...Okay, yes...Lyric williams...Room 119. My mom's eyes widened with relief. "Thank you," she said quickly.

But before they could head to my room, the nurse stopped them. "Wait... her brother is already back there with her," she said vaguely.

My mom's eyes narrowed suspiciously, "Her brother? This is the only brother that she has! The nurse paused and dropped her head, and my mom exchanged a skeptical glance with my brother. Something didn't add up.

And then they heard it.. "COLD BLUE ROOM 119. WE NEED ALL NURSES STAT" the voice on the hospital speaker said. Mom panicked asking,

"What's going on? Is it my daughter? Somebody fucking tell me something." she screamed.

That's when she turned and looked down the hall, she saw a man walking from my room wearing a fitted cap. Mom squinted up her eyes because she couldn't see at first and then widened her eyes and realized who the person was and said… "MARCO!"